THE
CORRUPTIONS
A JACK MARCONI THRILLER

VINCENT ZANDRI

The following is a work of fiction. Names, characters, places, events and incidents are either the product of the author's imagination or used in an entirely fictitious manner. Any resemblance to actual persons, living or dead, is entirely coincidental.

ISBN 978-1-943818-37-2

eISBN 978-1-943818-51-8

Library of Congress Control Number: 2016952316

First hardcover edition January 2017 by Polis Books, LLC

1201 Hudson Street, #211S

Hoboken, NJ 07030

www.PolisBooks.com

POLIS BOOKS

For Laura

"I hope I can make it across the border."

—Stephen King, Rita Hayworth and The Shawshank Redemption

What follows is based on fact. Some of the names have been changed for legal purposes and/or to protect the innocence of the individuals to which they belong.

CHAPTER 1

Clinton Maximum Security Correctional Facility

Dannemora, NY

20 miles south of the Canadian Border

Present Day

Little Siberia.

It's what the three thousand inmates call this iron house...this frigid stoney lonesome. What they started calling it not long after the stone walls were first erected back in 1844 when the inmates were forced to work the local iron mines for ten hours a day, six days a week, until their shackled ankles bled, their hands blistered, and their lungs turned to black from iron ore dust.

The mines are gone now, but the relentless cold has decided to stay on, like a stiff, icy, iron hard-on. A reminder of the life and death that awaits you as soon as you enter the prison gates for the strip-searched, full anal cavity check primary indoctrination. Some of the New York State Historic Landmark's old stone walls remain as a visitor center showcase, while several new and improved cell blocks constructed of prefabricated concrete panels now house the majority of the hard-core inmates. The blocks are set inside castle-like, razor-wire topped reinforced concrete walls protected by strategically positioned guard towers manned by teams of riot shotgun and M16 packing corrections officers.

Without the mod con benefits of an efficient heating system, the upstate New York winters can be harsh and deadly in Little Siberia. At night, an inmate will gnash his teeth. He'll toss and turn and shiver on his rack in the relentless cold. He'll dream of sandy beaches, sultry summer nights, and cold, refreshing bottles of beer. But when he wakes up, a layer of frost will coat his blanket.

But the torture doesn't end there. The real cold that invades your bones hasn't got shit to do with the weather. The real cold comes from the sounds of the inmates who surround you. Their crying. Their sobbing. Their moaning. Or maybe you'll hear them pleasuring themselves under their blankets, the sound of skin slapping skin, bruising your already shattered imagination. Or maybe two cellmates have married, and you've got no choice in hell but to swallow the squeaking of springs and a metal bed stand pounding the concrete block wall that separates your cell from theirs. You shiver from the dark, cold loneliness and you listen for the boot steps of the black-uniformed, ballistic-vested screws who pass by every fifteen minutes for yet another head count, and you think about the woman you left behind while you do a twenty-five to life stint. Sure, she writes you, calls you, and even visits on occasion. But in your frozen brain you can't help but see her slipping off sheer satin panties while wrapped in the arms of another man, maybe your best friend, her manicured hand running up his thigh until she finds exactly what she wants. Exactly what she's been missing.

That's the life you lead in Little Siberia, which isn't really life at all, but an existence of sorts, until parole comes your way or you die. Either way, you get the hell out. But getting out can take a long time. An eternity. A time so long that many men have gone insane, going to their deaths a sniveling, white-haired, toothless shadow of their former selves.

But for two inmates, Reginald Moss, a stocky, black-haired forty-something white man doing life for murder one and his cellmate, Derrick Sweet, a skinny, pale, nervous thirty-something former computer geek who's also doing a homicide-mandated life sentence, waiting it out until insanity and death embraces them is no longer an option. Instead they choose freedom.

They choose escape.

The prison and surrounding forest are still cold even in early June, with night temperatures sometimes plunging into the thirties or forties.

"Fuck, it's cold," Sweet says, pulling up the collar on his prison green work shirt, as if the act will make an ounce of difference. "Those global warming freaks are full of shit."

"Shut up and work," Moss says, sawing away at the horizontally-mounted main sewer line located behind their cell.

"You're a fucking robot, you know that, Picasso?" Sweet says, working his own blade on the same pipe so that the square opening they're about to complete will allow both their frames access to the pipe's interior. "What kind of human being dismembers his boss, huh? You're a fucking psycho, you know that? Psychopath-robot-Picasso…that's you, my friend."

Moss looks up. His eyes blink only when he wants them to. And right *now, he's not giving them permission.*

"You shot a sheriff's deputy twenty-two times," he says in his monotone drawl, his slicked back hair held perfectly in place, making his full face even fuller, his thick neck even thicker. "You then ran him over with your pickup. Like he wasn't already roadkill. Like his face wasn't entirely shot away, his brains already blown out the back of his skull. Who are you to call me a psycho? Psycho."

Sweet chomps down on his bottom lip, runs his hand over his cropped scalp, and down his trim mustached and goateed face. While his Adam's apple bobs up and down inside his long turkey neck, his big brown eyes grow even wider, like one of those little rubber toys you squeeze with your fist to make the eyes bulge out.

"Fucker had it comin', bitch. I mean, he was a cop. All cops got it comin', you know? Got it comin' one way or the other. Filthy bastards. Whadda we want? More dead cops. I like the way Obama keeps pissin' on 'em. He's got my vote next election." Mulling over what he's just said for a moment, as if digesting words of brilliance. Then, shrugging his shoulders, "Can we vote for US president in Mexico?"

"Obama's already done his eight years, imbecile," Moss says.

But Sweet ignores his partner, shakes his head. "God, it's fucking cold."

Then, the abrupt clang of a square metal section of pipe dropping onto another section of pipe.

Both men lock eyes like, What the fuck!

They stand stone stiff, knowing that sounds, especially metal against metal, can reverberate throughout the concrete prison block with all the alarming concussion of a lightning strike. Time ticks by…tick, tick, tick.

After a few beats, Moss wipes his brow with the back of his hand.

"*Be more careful, for Christ's sakes, Sweet,*" *he whispers, his voice harsh but controlled. "This is our one and only shot. Mean Gene might be looking out for us. But I think he's having second thoughts about helping us. Won't take much for him to renege on his promise to keep the screws away from our cell tonight.*"

Sweet pictures the tall corrections officer who's not only taken a liking to Moss over the years, but who's been paying them both in favors for information on other inmates and, even more importantly, other COs working deep down inside the Crypt. Mean Gene has also adopted an appreciation for Moss's artwork, often trading gifts of food and other luxuries for one of Moss's oil paintings.

Sweet blows Moss a kiss, which Moss ignores. Instead, both men look into the dank blackness of the pipe interior.

"*Jeeze, it smells bad, Picasso,*" *Sweet says. "Think I'm gonna gag. Then I'm gonna puke all over my work boots.*"

"*You can gag a free man or you can sleep here tonight and tomorrow night and all the nights after that 'til you die.*" *Cocking his head in the direction of the cell, he says, "Grab our stuff and let's go.*"

"*Why I always gotta take your orders, Picasso?*"

"*'Cause I like it that way. And I'm older than you. And smarter.*"

"*The sensitive artist. You're stuck up, you know that? You think you're better than everyone. You and that paint brush and that cock of yours...just ask Mean Gene.*"

Moss has got a choice here. He could grab the framing hammer that's set on its head on the floor and jam the business end through the skinny punk's forehead. He could bash the kid's brains in in the time it takes to say Merry fucking Christmas. He might then spit down into the bloody mess, drop the body off the catwalk into the no man's land between cell blocks, and make the great escape all on his own. But instead, he chooses to suck it all up and force a smile. It's a small smile. A Mona Lisa smile. A smile that's more common coming from one of the prison screws. Or so it seems. But he smiles the smile of a man who is about to be free of this place and free of homicidal whack-jobs like Derrick Sweet. Besides, as much as he hates the bastard, he needs a second pair of eyes to back him up. At least until they are far away from Dannemora and under the cover of the great Adirondack wilderness and the deep night.

"Yeah, well, you've used that ten-inch cock to our advantage, Picasso, I gotta give you that," Sweet remarks. "Let's just hope Blondie is Janey-on-the-spot with the ride as soon as we get through that manhole cover."

Moss pictures the small blonde woman he's been bedding down with inside Tailor Shop Number 1 for a few years now. The voice inside him says, Yeah, it pays to have friends on the inside. Pays to have a killer porno cock too.

"She prefers Joyce, her real name, and don't forget the deal, Sweet. We pay her husband a visit while he sleeps in his bed and then we head south for Mexico."

"Yeah, I haven't forgotten the deal." *He puckers up his nose again.* "Can we just go now already, Picasso?"

"Go get the shit. And don't forget to set the painting back in place when you come back out."

"Yeah, fucking, yeah already, I know the drill, Picasso."

"And stop calling me Picasso. Van Gogh is more my style." *He pronounces Van Gogh in the formal manner. Like Van Gock.*

Sweet backs away from the pipe, about-faces, steps back up onto the metal catwalk that accesses the electrical utility boxes. He finds the back of their cell, the four-by-four hole they've cut through the wall concealed by a piece of cardboard painted a dull gray to mimic the painted concrete block. Grabbing their single laundry duffel and the few items of clothing and homemade weapons it contains, he makes a quick check on the bunks, both of which are stuffed with clothing and fake papier-mâché heads, making it look like the two inmates are fast asleep, just like that old Clint Eastwood Escape from Alcatraz movie he watched on Youtube in the library. Satisfied their plan is proceeding as well as can be expected, the nervous man once more pushes the fake wall aside and slips on through onto the catwalk. Replacing the wall, he approaches Moss.

"Got the shit," he says, reaching into the duffel, producing their one and only flashlight, "Can we go now, Picasso? I'm freezing and I wanna get this shit over with."

Moss is still staring down into the hole, not like he's inspecting the pipe. More like he's looking into his future. Both immediate and beyond. Like he's seeing the beaches of Mexico, feeling the warmth on his skin, a cool drink in one hand and a paintbrush in the other. But first, he's got to squeeze himself through this asshole of a sewer pipe, crawl through its metal, shit-lined intestines, and pooped out the other end.

"Let's do it," he says. Then, "Oh, and, Sweet? No bitching, you hear me? We maintain absolute silence all the way through. That clear? And like we planned, no flashlight until we're beyond the prison walls."

Sweet smiles, bearing crooked, gray teeth beneath tiny, overly thin lips.

"Yeah, Picasso," he says, running his free hand nervously over his short stand of receding black hair. "Sweet idea. Get it?" He follows with a snort, like it's the first time he ever used the silly quip instead of the millionth.

"You first," Moss says. "Like we talked about. I get stuck, you don't want me blocking your way. You'll suffocate to death." But the painter is also thinking this: I'm older than you. Out of shape. I don't wanna slow you down. Yeah, he might wanna kill Sweet sometimes, but other times it pays to be considerate. He can use all the good karma he can muster up, given the crappy circumstances he's currently faced with.

Suddenly Sweet's smile disappears. Tossing in the duffel, he crouches and slips his entire torso down into the pipe, headfirst, like he's entering into an MRI machine, only narrower, tighter, longer, smellier…

"God, I'm gonna puke," comes his muted voice.

"Shut up and get going," Moss says, assuming a crouched position as soon as Sweet has started his crawl into the pitch blackness. He's about to place his round head into the pipe when he remembers something. Reaching into the chest pocket on his work shirt, he pulls out a Post-it-Note. Neatly illustrated on the little square slip of yellow paper is what bigots used to refer to as a Chinaman, the face smiling, eyes sloped down towards the slit-like nose, a triangular bamboo hat set precariously on the round face's head like the bad cliché that it is. Below the face, "Have a nice day!" is scrawled in happy-go-lucky Crayola Crayon handwriting.

Moss sticks the note onto the pipe beside the newly sawed opening, and for what feels like the first time since he entered Little Siberia years ago, he issues a short, nearly noiseless laugh. A laugh meant entirely for his own enjoyment. A laugh in the face of the rank shit stink rising up from the pipe like a poison gas. A laugh in the face of the screws who beat him and forced him to work down inside the Dannemora Crypt, making movies with little kids barely more than a decade old. A laugh in the face of the man who is sleeping with his wife in Mexico…a man who *will soon be dead. A laugh only the devil himself could understand while slipping under red satin sheets, lighting a cigarette, and pouring a snifter of brandy. A laugh befitting of a cold, evil son of a bitch.*

CHAPTER 2

Albany, New York

60 Hours Later

I was debating whether or not to eat the second half of my Italian combo with extra provolone submarine when the goons walked in without knocking. They were big. Bigger than my five feet ten, and chestier. Not like gym rats but more like chronic roid users. Muscles for show rather than the smaller but more utilitarian muscles I worked on in the Albany Strength gym five days a week. Mine weren't nearly as glamorous or tough looking. But they worked the way I expected them to on those occasions when I was required to punch someone, or be punched, and that was just fine by me.

The first goon, a black man whom I took for the leader, shot me a look from underneath a pair of sleek wrap-around Rayban sunglasses. He was wearing a dark blue suit with a matching blue tie and a gray button-down shirt underneath. His shorter, whiter, but just as stocky partner wore an identical suit, shirt, tie, and sunglasses. Both of them had earbud wireless radio devices shoved in their left ear canals so that they could communicate with whoever was monitoring them from the outside. My guess was they thought they looked Jason Bourne-cool and that other people were in awe, if not fear, of them. I thought they looked like funeral directors.

As they searched the room with their eyes, turning every now and then on the balls of their feet, I just hoped they didn't decide to search my sandwich. I was still hungry after all.

"Can I help you, gentlemen?"

The taller one shot me another crooked glance. No response.

"Someone die?" I said.

Tall Goon gave Short Goon a look like I wasn't supposed to say that. Or it wasn't in their script anyway.

"What?" Tall Goon said. "Who said anything about anyone dying?"

I sat far back in my grandfather's old hand-me-down swivel chair, worked up a friendly smile. "You look like funeral home directors."

Short Goon bit down on his bottom lip. "He's being an asshole, Stanley. Told you everyone thinks he's an asshole. He must have learned that shit when he was warden at Green Haven. The boss ain't gonna like him. Thinks he's a know-it-all. Know what I'm sayin', Stanley?"

"Forget him and concentrate on the job, Brent," Stanley said.

"Who called me a know-it-all?" I said. "I just wanna finish my lunch."

Tall Goon/Stanley completed his search of the room. Apparently satisfied that I didn't have a bomb rigged up for his boss or that I wasn't hiding a Fox News reporter in the corner or that the place wasn't bugged for sound, he made for the door and waved whoever was hidden behind the wall to come in.

When the suited man came through the door, Brent and Stanley took their places beside the open door. Each of them unbuttoned their jackets, allowed them to open just enough for me to make out the black grips on their service automatics.

Intimidating.

The half sandwich set before me smelled good. I didn't want to be talking to clients right now no matter how important they were. I'd made the commitment to eating the second half of my sandwich and damnit, that's what I was going to do.

The important client pulled one of the two wood chairs I reserved for visitors closer to my desk and sat down.

"Do you know who I am?" he said.

Of course I recognized him. Everybody in New York State government knew his name. You'd have to be living under a rock not to know his face and name and political persuasion. But then, I guessed some people steered clear of politics. They knew who Bruce Caitlyn Jenner was, and who Lady Gaga was, and they even knew the precise dimensions of Kim Kardashian's ample behind. But not who their own governor was.

I stared at the rest of sandwich. It screamed, *Eat me!* in a nice way.

"Provolone," I said.

"Excuse me?"

The Governor had dressed himself in a tailored summer-weight tan jacket, also tailored dark trousers and before he sat down I noticed his loafers were Gucci. Because he represented the left bank of the Democratic Party, he didn't wear a tie. His one concession to the blue collar Marxist revolution crowd. But he wasn't fooling anybody, because the silk jacket cost more than my entire wardrobe of two blue blazers, half a dozen Converse button down shirts, three pairs of Levis 501 button flies, and two pairs of Tony Lama cowboy boots.

"Provolone cheese," I said, staring down at my lunch. "Did you know that it comes from Casilli near Mount Vesuvius? It was a staple of the inhabitants of Pompeii."

He stuffed his tongue in his cheek, looked at me with intense, unblinking eyes.

"No," he said. "I was not aware."

"You should be as an Italian American."

"Italian and Libyan, if you must know the truth. Mother and father, respectively."

"Interesting combination. You can enjoy your pasta in the desert. *Manga Allahu Akbar*, so to speak."

I saw the eyes on Stanley go wide, even if they were masked by sunglasses. He set his shooting hand on his pistol grip. Made me tremble with fear.

"Listen, Mr. Marconi—"

"Keeper. Call me Keeper, your majesty."

Stanley took a step forward. "You watch your fuckin' mouth, pal. That's the Honorable Leon Valente to you." More tickling of the holstered pistol.

"Your boys like their guns, I see," I said. "Thought you wanted to abolish the second amendment."

"Evil necessity, the very outdated United States Constitution."

I patted my rib cage where my .45 rested. "I'm quite fond of my Colt 1911. Makes me feel warm and cozy and free."

"Governor will be fine," the governor said.

"Excuse me?"

"You wished to know how to address me. So I'm telling you." Then, over his shoulder. "That will be enough, Stanley. Please take your hand off your sidearm."

Stanley resumed his solid foursquare position up against the wall, the dejection painting his face in the form of red blood blush.

"I see that I've interrupted your lunch," Valente went on. "But what I have to reveal is of the utmost importance."

"You want a bite?"

He cracked a grin. "I don't eat that kind of thing. Pork products especially."

"You Jewish?"

His face was permanently tan. But it turned red at the mere suggestion.

"I believe in God," he said under his breath. "That's about as far as it goes."

"You probably have a dietician. Someone who cooks for you. At taxpayer expense, of course. Karl Marx had a cook. So did Uncle Joe Stalin. And Obama. Perks for the public servant."

He cocked his head, as if to say, *It comes with the gig.* "I like to keep fit. Box mostly. You keep fit too, I see."

"I run and lift. Or they used to call it running and lifting, until they decided to call it cross-training. Now they call it cross-fit. Tomorrow they'll call it something else like trans-fit. Something that won't insult anybody who wants to dispose of their penis."

"Political correctness is all about human evolution, Keeper," he said proudly, like he invented it. "It's the essence of progressivism."

"I'd rather talk about maxing out on a flat bench."

"Stanley and Brent can bench three hundred pounds." He smiled, like he was responsible for that too.

The two goons nodded proudly.

"Collectively?" I said. "Or individually?"

Valente cleared his throat, crossed his legs.

"Individually," he said, exasperation in his tone. "Listen," he added, glancing at his gold wristwatch. "Time is tight."

"I imagine it is, your greatness," I said. "So, how can I be of service?"

Any semblance of a smile was now gone. He looked at me like I was playing some kind of joke on him on the school playground for the entire student body to see. His concave-cheeked face was steely, taut, as if it might explode blood and brain matter all over my sandwich. That would kind of suck. No, that would suck a lot.

"Dannemora Prison," he said, rubbing his pug nose with his fist, kind of like he wanted to pick it with his thumb. But knowing I was watching him, he couldn't risk it. "There's been an external breach."

"You don't say?"

"Don't you look at the news?"

"I have a smartphone. Does everything but make my lunch. For that I still have to hoof it to Frank's Deli over on Albany Shaker in the North End."

We both focused in on my sandwich. I think he actually wanted a bite but was too afraid to admit it. Or too proud over his pork boycott. He was clean shaven, his hair natty and curly and dyed jet black. His skin was tan, but somehow pale, like coffee with way too much milk in it. And the way his dark, almost black marble eyes peered at me made him look like he could be related to the late Libyan dictator, Moammar Khadafy. Who knows, maybe Moammar was his great uncle.

"Two dangerous murderers are on the loose in Upstate and I need them apprehended. Yesterday, if you get my drift." His accent didn't originate from Albany, or anywhere from Upstate for that matter, but was instead Manhattan born. What it meant was that he pronounced his consonants with all the force of a Mike Tyson uppercut.

"I saw you on the news with the state troopers a few days ago. You said you were gonna find them in a matter of hours. Been a matter of hours now. And days. Two full days, I think."

He nodded, his Adam's apple bobbing up and down. "The escaped are nefarious."

"Does that word mean, like, sly and cunning, Herr Valente?"

Stanley took a step forward, his hands balled into fists.

"Stanley!" Valente shouted. "I'll handle this." Then, raising up his right hand he made like a pistol, pointed it at my face, poked the air with his index finger. He looked one way and then the other, like he was expecting The New York Times to show up at any moment. "You… you are a fucking wise ass, you know that?"

He lowered his hand and uncrossed his legs, sitting himself up straighter.

"Sorry," I said. "Semi-empty stomach and all. Just dying to get back at those pork products."

He cleared his throat again. "So then, back to finding the two men who've escaped—"

"Moss and Sweet," I interjected.

"Yes, Reginald Moss and Derrick Sweet. Finding them hasn't been easy. The state troopers are stymied and now the Feds are threatening to join in the hunt."

"Plus the Canadian Mounted Police, the US Marshalls, and the border patrol—land, sea, and air divisions." I held up my smartphone.

"See, I keep up with the news."

"I'm not concerned with the Canadians. They'll do whatever I say. I'm concerned with my state police since they're leading the ground search. And frankly, Mr. Marconi, it annoys the crap out of me that the lead trooper, short guy by the name of D'Amico, refuses to abide by my directives."

"D'Amico," I said. "I've seen him on the news. Short, intense guy. Reminds me of a fireplug, minus the red paint."

"Everything's under control. Relatively speaking. Even if D'Amico claims it's not."

"Something in the news about you refusing to share a press conference with D'Amico," I added. "Also you won't share the podium with the Clinton County Sheriff, who I believe is a woman and a looker at that. Gee, that's gotta hurt their feelings."

He cracked a grin. "I like to run my show my way, without First Deputy Superintendent D'Amico's or Sheriff Hylton's interference."

"But aren't you all in bed together? Situationally speaking, of course."

"They do things their way," he said like I was talking about his ex-wife, who if I remembered correctly, was a distant cousin of the Kennedys. You know, like, from *the* Kennedy family. "I do my thing my way, and my thing is the most important thing because I'm ultimately responsible for the safety of every single New Yorker."

"*Capisce*," I said.

"What?" he said.

"You should have followed up your *my way* speech with *Capisce*. It would have sounded better. More forceful. So what is it you want from me, Don Valente?"

Commotion coming from the office door. "Son of a—"

"Stanley!" the governor barked once more. His eyes were back on me. "You used to run a prison before becoming a PI. You know prisons, how they work, or in this case, don't work. You know inmates, what makes them tick. So far we've come up with nothing. No leads. Not a thing. Not even after offering a reward of one hundred grand has produced so much as a fingerprint."

I nodded. "Why the personal approach? Don't you have more pressing matters on your plate? Like dismantling the NRA or something?"

He leaned towards me.

"Listen," he said. "There hasn't been an escape from Dannemora ever in its one hundred sixty years of existence, and a cop killer hasn't escaped a New York State joint in nineteen years. You should know that because that killer escaped from your prison, and you apprehended him."

"Dead," I said. "When I got to him he was dead. Then the good guys wanted me to die for it too. But that's another story."

"These guys get a hold of some weapons, they could go on a killing spree that would make ISIS look like the Boy Scouts. And guess who's gonna get the brunt of the blame?"

"Oh yes," I said. "That little problem with prison funding in this year's budget. Staff layoffs. Too many prisoners, too few corrections officers to monitor the stoney lonesome."

"Well, I'm not gonna let these killers get away. Not gonna let that happen on my watch."

"Plus there's the little bit about your putting your foot in your mouth by saying you'll recover them in twenty-four hours."

"Okay, yeah, I bit off more than I can chew, which is why I'm calling you in and why no one's gonna know about it."

Once more I looked at the second half of my sandwich. I hoped it still loved me as much as I loved it.

"That is if I take the job," I said. "If I do, whom shall I report to, your governance?"

He shook his head. "No respect for a political authority."

"That's not true," I said. "We all lie from time to time. You guys just do a hell of a lot more of it." Raising up my head, I shouted, "Stanley!"

"Just give me the word, Governor Valente," the goon said, "and I will be happy to teach Mr. Marconi a lesson he won't soon forget."

"Uh-oh," I said. "I think I pooped myself."

"Look," Valente interjected, "it's possible these guys could already be in Mexico."

I shook my head. "Unlikely. They're probably within twenty miles of the joint. Those woods are thick and they're on foot from what I'm reading. Probably bunkered down somewhere until the heat is off them."

"How can you be sure?"

"Escaped convicts usually want one thing. To get laid. After that they just want a cold beer and a hot meal."

"Moss already did time in Mexico. His south-of-the-border-señorita wife has shacked up with a new guy. Sweet is unattached and a bit of a wild man, or so I'm told. I'm placing my bets on them trying to get to Mexico."

"Who helped them on the inside?"

"We got a woman, Joyce Mathews, worked in the tailor shop. She's been balling them both in between stitches, so to speak. We think she helped smuggle in some tools. Screwdrivers, hacksaws, power tools she lifted from the construction going on inside the place. She also promised them a ride out of town as soon as they got free. But she got cold feet, feigned an anxiety attack, and ended up going to the emergency room."

"Where's she now?"

"Clinton County Jail."

"Motivation? And don't tell me it's love."

"Don't quote me on this but I think Moss and Sweet agreed to kill her husband, Larry, if she agreed to arrange transport."

"Now that makes perfecto sense," I said, pulling a yellow legal pad from the top desk drawer, writing down Joyce's name along with her husband's. "Anyone else?"

"There's a corrections officer," Valente said. "Name of Gene Bender. Inmates call him Mean Gene because he's big and bad ass, and plays bass guitar in a hardcore band."

"He must also be a boxer like you."

"Funny," he said. "He's in the process of being read his Mirandas for aiding and abetting. He's on his way to Clinton County lockup also."

"What'd he do exactly?"

"Like Joyce, he slipped some tools in along with some raw meat for the two escapees. Claims he developed a relationship with them in exchange for info on other inmates."

"Seems reasonable enough. I would have done the same thing. But raw meat?"

"They'd earned time in the honor block and they were allowed to cook some of their own meals."

I nodded. Little known fact about max security prisons. Honor block prisoners could cook their own meals, keep their own gardens, and even earn conjugal visits from time to time. I jotted down Mean Gene's name. I also jotted down, *Tools hidden in raw meet. Dumb rookie mistake.*

"Who you want me to answer to? D'Amico?"

He shook his head. "The aforementioned Bridgette Hylton. That's Hylton with a Y."

I wrote that down too, including Hylton's Y.

"Dannemora Super?"

He told me and I scribbled the name, Peter Clark. In my heart of hearts, I knew that not only would Warden Clark lose his Christmas bonus, he was about to lose his job.

Valente stood, smoothed out his pants. He was a dapper leftist governor who was, at present, single, and he took pride in both, from what the tabloids reported. The New York Post anyway. That and his boxing and his bodyguards. Excuse me, Secret Service.

"And I'm sure all of these good people are sharing their information."

He cocked his head.

"Bureaucrats," he said, his voice filled with as much irony as my provolone and pork product-filled sub.

"Politicians," I said. Then, "Assuming you are my client and not necessarily the State of New York, who would you like me to speak to first?"

"I think you'll do well to start with Sheriff Hylton. She's more reasonable than D'Amico."

"Looks like all roads lead to Hylton," I said. "Hylton with a Y, that is."

"Please stop that," he said. "We heard it the first time."

Both Stanley and Brent snorted, as if it was specifically spelled out in their contracts to snort whenever their boss made a funny.

"You got a file for me to, ummm, peruse?" I asked.

"You've got yourself a smartphone and a news app or two," he said. "Use them."

Another pair of snorts from the Lurch twins. This time it was me who made a pistol with my right hand. When I pointed it at the governor, I said, "Touché."

He reached into his jacket, pulled out an envelope, handed it to me.

"Advance," he said. "I'm sure it's adequate."

"I'll take your word for it, Governor."

"Of course you will," he said, turning. He started walking. But he stopped just short of the door and the monsters who guarded it. "Oh, and if you would be so kind, Mr. Marconi," he added, "if and when you happen to discover one or both of our missing prisoners, make certain you contact me on my private cell phone immediately. I want them both front and center, and I want them alive. You got that? Alive. That's the kind of compassionate governor I am. You understand?"

I nodded. "Number?"

"It's in the envelope along with the check."

"Gee, thanks. Now I have goosebumps."

"You don't really mean that."

"Spoken like a true politician."

Even he had to laugh at that one. He turned and exited the door, followed by the two goons.

I sat back down, tossed the envelope aside, grabbed up my sandwich with both hands.

Hell knoweth no fury like a starving gumshoe.

CHAPTER 3

My sandwich was now a bitter sweet memory. Sweet because it tasted great. Bitter because it was all gone. I cleaned up the mess and tossed the trash into the metal waste can under my desk. My hands were greasy. So I made my way out of the old former 1920s and '30s downtown Albany, Sherman Street garment factory office, down the narrow corridor to the washroom.

Opening both the hot and cold spigots on the old white porcelain sink, I took a good look at myself in the mirror. At the somewhat rounded face that supported a salt and pepper goatee that matched closely the head of cropped hair that didn't seem to be receding as fast as I once thought. For ages I contemplated pulling out the razor, going Bruce-Willis-bad-ass on my scalp, but then thought better of it since I'd probably end up looking like a cue ball with whiskers.

I still had hair after all. So why not flaunt it?

I looked into my brown eyes. Eyes that were still bright. Still optimistic. A far cry from what they once were back when I was the warden at Green Haven, and my life was turned upside down, not only by the hit-and-run that killed my wife, Fran, but also by the escape of a cop killer right out from under my nose. The then acting Commissioner of Corrections laid the blame squarely on my size forty four shoulders, which meant one of two things. I could either face prison time myself inside my own joint…a situation which, when translated, meant a sure death sentence. Or, I could go after the killer on my own, bring him back in on my own terms rather than risk him getting away for good.

A splash of cold water on my face.

It came back to me then. The desperate feeling of knowing a cop killer has just walked out the front door of your prison, so to speak. I knew exactly how the warden of Dannemora felt right now. How desperate he must be. If he'd been experiencing night sweats and tremors over the past two nights. I wondered if he'd slept at all, or if he spent most of his time pacing the floors, questioning himself, wondering precisely where he went wrong. I wondered how many phone calls he'd already ignored from the commissioner. From Governor Valente. Phone calls from state police, the federal marshals, the FBI, from Sheriff Hylton. Phone calls from the news, both local and national.

I wondered how much he was drinking. Smoking. Drugging. Trying to douse the pain that burned like a flame inside his belly.

Most of all, I wondered how badly he wanted to run away.

Pulling a handful of paper towels from the dispenser, I dried my face and discarded the used towels into the trash receptacle. On my way out of the bathroom, I once more caught my eyes staring back at me in the mirror. I stopped and gazed into them. But something else also drew my attention. The paper towel I'd just discarded. I could see it in the mirror, resting atop the rim of the wall-mounted dispenser. The wet, crumpled paper resembled a face. Or, not a face necessarily, but a profile. It was a strange if not eerie play of light and shadow miraculously distributed onto the paper towel to create a 3D face. In the mirror, I could make out the eyes, the long nose, the lips, and a chin that might have been covered with a beard. It was a white face. A white face that reminded me of Christ.

I wanted to laugh. Because who the hell saw the face of Jesus in a used paper towel? The same kind of people who saw his face in a grilled cheese sandwich, I guessed. But then, it wasn't very funny. Turning, I went to the dispenser and shoved the paper towel back down inside.

Turning back to the mirror, I once more caught my reflection.

"Sure you wanna take this job on?" my eyes said. "Sure you wanna open up all those old wounds? Maybe Paper Towel Jesus was trying to send you message, Keeper. Stay away from this one. It will cost you. Physically, emotionally."

I exhaled, nodded.

"Oh Christ," I said aloud inside the small ceramic tiled bathroom. "I'm not sure what to do." I shook my head. "Yes, you do. You know exactly what to do. A couple killers are on the loose, and some innocent people might need your help, Jack. The warden of Dannemora Prison needs your help. The sheriff needs it too. The escape isn't their fault, right?" I sighed. "Well, I guess we'll see about that."

"That settles it, then," said the voice inside my brain. "What's right is right until it's not right anymore."

I turned away from the mirror, faced the paper towel receptacle. I knew that Jesus was inside of it.

"There but for the grace of God I go," I said. And then I walked out.

CHAPTER 4

I f I was going to go after the escaped killers, I would need a little more background info on the prison, the town of Dannemora, the warden, the whole Department of *Corruptions* ball of wax. That meant I could either spend the day researching on the internet or I could bring in the help of an expert. Someone who knew prisons as well as I did. But not from the point of view of a CO or a keeper like me, but from that of an inmate.

Blood.

He agreed to meet me down on North Pearl Street at a bar called McGeary's, which was run by an affable and beautiful, long auburn-haired beauty named, Tess. Having managed a financial stake in several old Albany Bars, Tess was a highly regarded investor in Albany's much coveted happy hours. She was also somewhat of a local legend, her tall, shapely body always clothed in a long velvet dress, silver jewelry jangling on both wrists, long necklaces dangling from her neck, the pendants resting on her more than ample chest. It was a shame in a way that she preferred the fairer sex to that of my own, but I considered it my loss and some nice girl's gain.

She greeted me as soon as I came through the wood and glass door like she'd been expecting me the entire time. And with Blood already in the house, that might have been the case.

"You beautiful baby," I said, as I took her in my arms, kissed her luscious wet lips.

"You're right about that, Keeper Marconi," she said, when I released her. "And I'm proud to own it." She gave me a look, one eye open, the other closed. "Been a while since I've seen you."

I patted my belly. "Been trying to curb the carbs."

"Don't tell me you're switching to light beer. The world will never be the same."

I cocked my head. "Never. But I have been drinking a little more red wine these days."

"Fancy for a private dick. And Val approves of this move, no doubt." A question.

The Val she spoke of was my long-time, brunette-haired on again/ off again girlfriend and former Girl Friday from my days as warden. We'd nearly married once, but the ceremony ended before it began when my first wife's killer showed up in Albany. But that's another story for another time.

"Yes, Val approves." I didn't quite have the heart to tell her that Val and I weren't speaking right now. But I diverted her attention from my schizophrenic relationship by making a scan of the long barroom. I said, "So, is he here?"

Usually, you could feel Blood's presence without having to spot him. And today was no exception. Despite my inquiry, I could almost feel the big man's aura, like you might feel a ghost that's just passed through your skin, bone, and flesh.

Tess raised up her thumb, gestured over her shoulder.

"He's got a cold one waiting for you, darling," she said, making her way behind the antique bar. "No red wine for you today. Not in this joint."

I negotiated my way through the humble collection of summertime day drinkers until I came to the end of the bar where Blood was seated up on a stool. At six feet plus, he looked like a stone statue that had been hewn out of dark marble. He towered over me, but he never made me feel small. That was the kind of gift he had. A God given gift.

I sat down in the empty stool beside him, took hold of my Budweiser long-neck, stole a deep drink.

"That's okay," he said in his strong but almost monotone manner. "You don't have to say hello."

I set the bottle down and wiped the foam from my lips with the back of my hand.

"Question of priorities," I said. "I can either drink or talk. Which would you choose?"

He had a vodka martini set in front of him. Two green olives impaled on a toothpick lounging inside the clear, slightly cloudy liquid. Shaken not stirred, just like that other renowned slick 007 man of action and international intrigue preferred.

"Sometimes I think you borderline racist," he said, lifting his filled-to-the-brim glass slowly by the stem, not spilling a drop, taking a careful sip without making a sound. He set the glass back down and exhaled slowly. "Perfect. Tess knows her mixology."

"That she does," I said. "And I'm no racist. I'm sitting here with you right now, aren't I?"

"You just sitting here because you look more attractive to the ladies when you near me."

He had a point. Blood was a magnet for men who wanted to be him, and women who wanted to be *with* him. A former semi-pro Albany Metro Maulers football player and a former inmate at Green Haven Prison during my tenure, Blood was proof positive that a con could not only be reformed, but that once on the outside, could thrive. His crime, if you wanted to call it that, the one that put him away for seven to ten, involved the killing of a ruthless gangbanger who'd cut the throat of a teenaged girl he'd just raped inside a dark, damp back alley. If you were to ask Blood about it, which you most certainly should not, he would tell you he'd do it all over again.

Right is right, and wrong can be so dead wrong sometimes.

Nowadays, he presided like a king over most of upper Sherman Street where my home office was located, and even the cops asked his permission first before making a bust in that general vicinity. Today he was wearing his standard uniform of black jeans, boots, and black T-shirt which fit his sculpted muscles like a second skin. Blood was my gym rat partner not because it felt good being around him, but because he was something to physically aspire to.

His intellect was no slouch either. Having completed his undergraduate degree and earning an MA in English lit while in the can, he'd become a brilliant source of information and an even more brilliant researcher. He was also good with a gun, and unlike today's politicians and priests, he was physiologically incapable of telling a lie. It was quite possible that he was as close to perfection as God had come when he created man in his own image. And Blood knew it too.

"Glad you're available," I said, glancing over my shoulder at a small gathering of women, one of whom, a blonde, dressed in a dark blue mini skirt and matching jacket, had one blue eye locked on her stable of friends and another on Blood. I guessed it was possible she was looking at me, but if I were a betting man…

I cleared my throat. "Thought you might still be working as a research assistant for that writer, Reece Johnston," I said. "What's the title of his new book again? *Everything Burns*?"

"He finished with his new book. He's taking time off."

"Glad to hear it. You look into Dannemora?"

"You never got up there when you was bossing me around down in Green Haven?"

"No one went up there they didn't have to, Blood. It's north of Plattsburgh. Snows ten months out of the year I'm told."

He took another sip of his martini, then shot a hint of a smile at the blonde…a generous display of emotion for Blood. I thought she might melt.

"Not quite ten months out of the year, but close. Folks up there, prison and civies, call the place Little Siberia. Get this. Four thousand damaged souls live there, three thousand of them inmates. Some houses surround the prison walls. Nothing special. Constructed during the Second World War for the guards who watched over Nazi POWS incarcerated in the prison. Pretty much just a single main street that borders the joint. They got a Stewarts convenience store with three self-service gas pumps, a Price Chopper supermarket, a Dannemora Federal Credit Union for the Corrections Officers, a diner, a McDonald's, a Wendy's and a Chinese restaurant called Fangs. That's about it."

I stole another sip of beer. "What, no Burger King? No wonder those cons wanted out."

"Fast food? Not for those white boys. They was honor block. They cooked primo chopped sirloin on their own grill right up there on the cat walk."

"So I've heard. Security been lax up there?"

"Yup."

"Think that's why Governor Valente extended the personal touch, appealed to me personally with his merry band of goons?"

"Yup."

"He says it's an inside job. Think that's true?"

"Yup."

"Warden in a shitload of trouble, then."

"Yup."

"You ever say nope?"

"Yup."

I drank more beer. Finished the bottle. Blood drank down the rest of his martini. He held up the glass for Tess, and without so much as a syllable, persuaded her to drop what she was doing and begin making him another one. Over my shoulder, I once again glanced at the blonde bombshell. Both her blue eyes were now locked on Blood, like I didn't exist.

"How do you do it?" I said, not needing to explain myself further.

"It's a talent. You born with it."

"Must have been a bitch in the joint."

"Inmates knew better than to lay a horny hand on me. I knew better than to get in trouble on the outside again. Now I sitting here with you, my former super, employing me, drinking with me. Kibitzing with me. All worked out in the end, you dig?"

"You didn't just say, *you dig*?"

"Been watching more than my fair share of those '70s movies and television on Hulu. Blackula, Bruce Lee, Mod Squad. Stuff like that. People was cool back then. Used cool language and euphemisms."

Tess brought his martini and another beer for me. She blew each of us a kiss and patted my hand before she scooted back down to the other end of the bar.

"She like you," he said.

"She batting for the other team."

"Can't have it all ways. 'Sides, you got Val."

I coughed.

"Okay, you got Val now and again," he pointed out. "Mostly again. But me, I'm free as an eagle."

"And just as bald. Think we can find these two fence-jumping cons?"

"They went under the fence, and yes, they won't get far with you and me on their trail."

"Every law enforcement official from Plattsburgh to Canada is searching for them."

"I rest my case."

"What's the skinny on Moss?"

"Forty-nine. Loner. Killed his boss over a paycheck dispute. Dismembered the body. Also did time in a Mexican joint for murder over a drug deal gone bad. Smart, sensitive, but volatile. An artist. A good artist from the limited research I conducted in the single hour you gave me. Probably the brains behind the entire operation."

"Sweet?"

"The crazy one. Computer geek. The type who'd stay up for days and nights on end in his underwear, smoking meth and hacking into government servers. Shot a sheriff's dep not once, but twenty-two times. Reloaded three times. He then drove his pickup truck over him four or five times just because he could. Forensics had to ID the poor bastard by his teeth. Fucked up situation, you ask me."

"Dangerous. Think they're armed?"

"Lots of hunters from up that way. Most likely scenario is they found a cabin, broke into it, and found a weapon or two. Shotguns more than likely. Maybe .30-30s. Knives, axes, who knows what else."

"Most hunters would know better than to keep weapons lying around the cabins all summer long. Kids always bust into those places."

"Some of the hunters from New York City. Can't bring weapons back into Manhattan because of the Lincoln Laws. So they leave them upstate. Unlocked."

"You good with getting us some weapons besides sidearms? We're also going to need flashlights, bug spray, knives, tents, the whole kit and caboodle. Just in case we gotta camp out for a while."

"Caboodle?" he said. "What's a caboodle?"

"How should I know?"

"White people are strange. No wonder a black man president."

"The president is half white."

"Nobody's perfect."

"No truer words." Then, "Oh, before I forget."

Retrieving the envelope Valente passed on to me from the inside pocket on my blazer. I tore it open and pulled out the check.

"Sizeable," I said.

Blood leaned in, looked at the three zeros printed after the numeral 5. "Cover my costs anyway. For a few days."

"Good help will cost you," I said, sticking my fingers back inside the envelope once more, coming back out with a business card that had Valente's private cell number penned on it, and something else too. A yellow Post-it-Note upon which was scrawled a Chinese smiley face. Hand written below the face were the words, "Have a nice day!" with an exclamation point. The handwriting was cheerful and happy. Ironic.

"Now that's racist," Blood said. "Poor Chinese can't get no breaks."

I recognized the note right away from the television and online reports.

"It's the Post-it-Note Sweet and Moss left behind on the pipe beside the opening they cut out of it." Another drink of beer. "Why you suppose Valente included it in the envelope?"

"That's state's evidence. He must have had his reasons."

Pulling out my wallet, I folded the note and slipped it inside along with the check and business card. I finished my beer and Blood drained his martini. He also ate the two, now vodka-soaked, green olives.

"I think I'm ready for the woods," he said, sliding off the stool, standing tall, fit, and ready for anything. Even the blonde bombshell coming our way.

"Don't look now," I said, stepping aside, allowing her to enter our space.

"Got a date for tonight, big fella?" she said, a grin planted on her pretty face.

"You don't mess around with small talk do you, little lady?" Blood said.

She swayed slightly. "I'm a drittle lunk," she said. Then, giggling, "I mean, I a lunkle riddle...Oh crap, you know what I mean."

"I do," Blood said. He took her little hand in his, caressed it. "Sadly, I'm on my way to work. But another time perhaps."

He then leaned down and kissed her gently on the cheek. I thought she'd faint, so I made ready by standing foursquare behind her. When he released her hand, he started for the door. Blonde Bombshell silently watched the black god exit the bar.

"I'm Keeper," I said after a beat, holding out my hand. "Keeper Marconi."

"How nice for you," she said, walking away.

CHAPTER 5

"There anymore peanut butter, Picasso?"

"No. How about you get off your ass, end this vacation now, and head to the Stop and Shop and get us some?"

Derrick Sweet shifts his head on the cot pillow so that he's looking up at Reginald Moss from only a foot and half above the concrete floor of the secluded underground bunker. His fingers jammed into the mostly empty Skippy smooth peanut butter jar, he chuckles.

"I'm resting. Recharging my batteries. We got a long walk ahead of us now that Joyce decided to shaft us...bitch that she is. And to think of all the time we spent servicing her. Don't seem right, Picasso." He tosses the empty plastic jar across the single room, 1950s era shelter. "By the way, you were kidding about the Stop and Shop run, right? I mean, that would be, like, stupid, right? Am I right?"

Moss crosses thick arms over barrel chest. His shoulders are stained shit brown from crawling through that pipe that led directly to the sewer main and eventually to a manhole that opened up onto Main Street in downtown Dannemora. The escape had gone off without a hitch. Except for one thing: Joyce Mathews and their getaway vehicle never showed.

"I knew that bitch didn't want her husband dead," he mumbles. "She caved, chickened out at the last minute and now we gotta either steal a car or go north to Canada. Only thing that's gone our way is the location of this shelter."

"Steal a car. That sounds like a better plan. Got my heart set on Mexico, Picasso."

Moss steps on over to an easy chair covered in a red and black-checked wool blanket. He grabs hold of one of two pump-action shotguns that rest up against it. He pumps the action, allows a #3 buckshot shell to enter into the chamber.

"The woods up there are crawling," he says. "Only a matter of time 'til they stumble on us. Way I see it is like this: we either hoof it back through the woods to Dannemora and find a car to steal, which is like entering back into the hornet's nest, or we find another town and steal a car there."

"Okay, Picasso," Sweet says from down on the cot, examining the nails on his fingers, "we can't go back home, so to speak. So where's the nearest town? Gnome, Alaska?"

Moss turns, approaches the far concrete wall which supports a large framed topo map of the six-million-acre Adirondack State Park. He studies it for a moment. Until he raises his right hand, index finger extended, and pokes an area to the direct east of the underground shelter.

"Willsboro," he says after a time.

"Never heard of it," Sweet says.

"There's a shocker," Moss says, his eyes glued to the small settlement nestled in the middle of thick woods, streams, lakes, and mountains. At *least that's the way it looks according to the map's brown, green, and blue topographical makeup.* "It's a long walk though. Woods are gonna be jam packed with cops and troopers. Better we travel at night."

Just then, the sound of muted voices. Several muted voices all talking over one another. The voices come to them via the air ducts that connect the shelter interior to the exterior up above.

Sweet sits up fast. "That what I think it is, Picasso?"

Shifting himself back to the easy chair, Moss grabs hold of the second shotgun.

"They're fucking coming," he barks. "Looks like we're going nowhere for now."

"So what do we do, then?"

"Maintain silence until I say otherwise."

"What's that mean?"

"It means shut the fuck up, asshole."

CHAPTER 6

Two hours including a stop at Dick's Sporting Goods later, we were driving north on the highway in my recently refurbished fire engine red Toyota 4Runner. It was mid-June so we had plenty of sunshine for a drive that would take us somewhere around three and a half hours from Albany. We were dressed in clothing better suited for the great outdoors than Albany's downtown concrete jungle.

Like any other day, I was wearing a pair of Levis jeans, but instead of cowboy boots for footwear, I had on a pair of Chippewa lace-up work boots with indestructible Vibram soles over wool socks, a black cotton T-shirt that bore the words *Bomb Squad* from a favorite thriller series of mine, an olive green work shirt over that, and finally, a waterproof windbreaker with lots of pockets for my smartphone, a compass, my combo walkie-talkie GPS finder, waterproof matches, toilet paper, water purifying pills, granola bars, a Swiss Army knife and other assorted necessities should I get lost in the woods for a few days.

I also carried a Colt .45 strapped to my chest and two extra magazines should I suddenly find myself needing to shoot a bear.

Blood carried the same gear I did, only he looked much cooler doing it. Excepting his black windbreaker, his outfit of black jeans and T-shirt looked almost identical to the one he might wear down on Sherman Street. We were also hauling in the back cargo area of the 4Runner, two AR-15 semi-automatic rifles and five hundred rounds of .223 caliber Remmington ammo, some freeze-dried food, a case of bottled spring water, a two-man tent, sleeping bags, cooking equipment, portable stove, an eight-inch fighting knife apiece, night vision devices, and a case of beer. If nothing else, we were up for a nice vacation away from it all in the great Adirondack Mountains.

But somehow, I knew this was going to be anything but. If the voice that seemed to be getting louder and louder inside my gut was any indication, we were up for more than just a hike in the woods. We were about to come face to face with two killers who, already being charged with life sentences for their separate murders, had absolutely nothing to lose.

We arrived in the small town of Dannemora just after eight p.m. Like Blood had said, there wasn't much to the place other than the giant walls of the penitentiary to the right side of Main Street as we entered it, and the small commercial establishments on the left, and beyond those the small suburb made mostly of ramshackle wood clapboard homes. You could feel the tension in the air, the same way you might feel the presence of an intruder standing at the foot of your bed in the middle of the night.

More than one front porch contained a man or woman holding a shotgun or rifle. The streets weren't by any means crowded, but several people were dressed in camo as if it were hunting season, holstered pistols plainly visible.

You asked me, this was a small town where people were scared. On edge. And when that happened, you could almost guarantee someone was going to get shot, one way or another.

We passed by the many network news mobile broadcasting trucks, the camera crews, producers, and glamorous on-the-spot reporters who lazily roamed the Dannemora Prison parking lot, smoking cigarettes, mobile phones pressed up against their ears, or simply pacing the asphalt lot, waiting for something disastrous to happen. Something that would boost their ratings and extend their contracts.

We pulled into the Super Eight Motel within eyeshot of the prison, exited the 4Runner, stretched out, and entered into the check-in office located at the far north end of the two-story motel-no-tell. Unlike the parking lot, which was full of cars and trucks belonging to the many reporters and cops who'd converged on the scene, the reception area was empty. I went up to the counter, slapped the bell. And waited.

Blood stood by my side. Taller. Bigger. More put together.

"Not many keys left," he said, referring to the pegboard mounted to the wall behind the counter, and the small hooks that supported the room keys which were almost entirely picked over.

"Only one left," I said.

"Hope there's two beds," he said.

"Don't tell me you're homophobic, Blood. Just last week the president lit the White House up in the colors of the rainbow to celebrate gay marriage."

"His house, his choice."

I laughed. "Blood, say it ain't true. You are homophobic."

"I don't care what anybody does between consenting adults behind closed doors. But I don't cross swords, you dig?"

I laughed some more. "I'll try to keep my teeny weeny package away from your Jimmy Dean pork sausage if worse comes to worse."

"I sleep on the floor worse comes to worse, Mr. Teeny Weeny."

A man appeared from out of the back office. He was Asian Indian, and small, and wearing black, square horn-rimmed glasses.

"Can I help you?" he said in a heavy Indian accent.

"We'd like a room," I said. "Preferably with two beds."

The clerk nervously pulled on the top button of his cotton cardigan sweater, cleared his throat, then turned to look at the board.

"You are together?" he said.

"We work together is all," Blood said.

"I'm sorry," he said, turning back to the keyboard. "But there are no more rooms. The entire town is sold out. Many apologies."

I turned to Blood. "I guess we could set up the tent in the park. Camp out."

Blood's eyes went wide. "I prefer civilization for as long as I can get it." Nodding to the final key hanging off the board. "What about that one?"

Again, the clerk nervously pulled on the button, smiled.

"I am sorry, sir," he said in his almost sing-song voice, "but that would be quite impossible. You see, that room is reserved."

"What?" Blood said, shifting his massive torso so that it hung over the counter and therefore over the little clerk. "Reserved for who? We here first. First come, first served. That's the law of the land."

The clerk cleared his throat once more, his eyes wide behind his glasses. "That room is for Mr. Anderson Cooper. He would be very disappointed if I were to give his room away."

"Anderson Cooper," I said. "The CNN guy."

"Reporter," Blood said. "CNN big shot."

Nodding, the clerk said, "You do not like CNN?"

"What I don't like," Blood said, "is Mr. Cooper acting like he more important than me."

"Blood," I said, "Mr. Cooper has a reservation. Let's go pitch the tent."

He turned to me.

"You getting soft," he said. Then, stretching his long frame over the counter, he reached out above the clerk's head and grabbed hold of the key.

"Please, sir!" the clerk shot back.

Blood planted his feet, pocketed the key in his jacket. Then he dug into his black jean's pocket, pulled out an impressive roll of bills.

"How much for the room?"

The clerk held up his hands. "Under normal circumstances, fifty for the night. Ten extra for towels and maid service."

Blood shaved three hundred off the stack, slapped it down onto the counter.

"That's for three nights. Not sure we staying that long since it's possible we heading into the woods for a time."

The clerk's eyes lit up as he looked one way and then the other, and pocketed the cash in his trouser pocket and therefore, under the table.

"How much Mr. Anderson Cooper paying?" Blood said.

"Fifty," the clerk said. "Per night. Corporate Amex."

Blood cracked a smile. "See, we better clients. You make a better profit on us. No credit, cash. Keep Uncle Sam out of it."

Blood pulled the key back out of his jacket pocket, about-faced, and walked out of the office.

"Thanks," I said to the clerk, turning for the door.

"Excuse me?" he said as I put my hand on the opener. "What shall I say when Mr. Cooper arrives?"

"Tell him the truth," I said over my shoulder, opening the door.

"What truth would that be?"

"That a man named Blood is currently staying in that room, and Blood doesn't cross swords."

Laughing on the inside, I walked out.

CHAPTER 7

The first-floor, far corner room housed two beds after all.

We tossed our packs on our respective beds, along with the weapons, the ammo, and the case of beer. The rest of the gear remained stored in the 4Runner.

"You think he being straight about a celebrity like Anderson Cooper taking this room?" Blood said, stealing a beer from the case, popping the top. "Or you think he trying to take us for some dough?" He drank some of the beer.

"If he took us...*you*...for some dough with that story, then he deserves the money." I grabbed one of the beers, opened it, drank. The cool, as opposed to cold, beer tasted good after the long drive.

He smirked. "Guess you right. Blood, taken in by a little Indian man."

"Don't let it bother you, Blood. Even super humans have their vulnerabilities."

"Superman could use a real drink," he said, sneering at his beer can like it was beneath him. And it was. "Some food too."

"How about that Chinese restaurant?" I said. "Fangs."

"Only restaurant in town not attached to a chain," Blood said.

"Should be full of interesting people. Some of whom we might like to speak to in the interest of pinning down our escaped cons."

"My guess is most people don't know shit. Especially the police."

"Come on, Blood," I said, draining my beer. "Let's go make some friends."

Since Fangs was located only a few hundred feet from the motel, we took it on foot to the many sounds of the prison leaking over the big concrete wall. Electronic buzzers sounding off, metal smashing against metal, tinny indiscernible voices blaring over loudspeakers. The prison was a living, breathing entity. The beating heart of Dannemora.

There were a lot a vehicles parked out front of Fangs, which told us business was booming these days for the Fang family. Soon as Blood and I entered into the single-story, wide open dining room, the entire crowd fell silent while turning to stare at us, size us up. As we stood side by side next to a tall table that held maybe a half dozen, plastic-coated menus and that was presided over by a short Chinese woman in her mid to late 70s, all you could make out was the piped-in Chinese music. Listening closely, I could tell the music was actually Christmas songs being performed on traditional Chinese instruments.

"Isn't that *Silent Night*, Blood?" I said, making out the twang of a Chinese harp and the sad bowing of a violin-like instrument.

"That it is," he said. "*Silent Night*...in June. Kinda makes me homesick."

"Maybe we've entered a time warp. Like that FOX series, *Wayward Pines*."

"Maybe it's the year 4045," he said. "Christmas time. Good to know there's a still Christmas in 4045."

Maybe a dozen tables filled the wide open, brightly lit space. Some long and others round. No booths. Two tables to our right were occupied by what looked to be reporters. You could tell by the many mobile cameras that rested on the floor and the amount of empty beer and wine bottles that sat on the table beside plates of Moo Goo Gai Pan, poo poo platters, bowls of shrimp low mein, pork chow mein, and wanton soup. One of the women sitting at the closer table was tall, with dirty blonde hair. Her Fox News T-shirt fit her snuggly. I recognized her from the local Albany Fox News affiliate. She caught my glance and smiled. For a split second I assumed she was smiling at Blood. But when I realized her happy face was devoted to me and me alone, I felt a wave of warmth shoot up my spine. I smiled back.

A couple more of the long tables were occupied by the state police. Their table was far more orderly, with soft drinks only on hand set beside their gray Stetsons. Sitting at the head of the closest table was a short, fit man, his hair brush-cut short, his grey and blue uniform impeccable. To his credit, he was the only man from the table not staring at us while he carefully sipped soup from a white ceramic spoon.

The long table beyond them was filled with big men dressed in uniform blues, the sleeves on their shirts rolled up, showing off bulging, HGH-fed biceps. The patches on their shirts revealed their occupation as corrections officers for the Empire State of New York. Their drinks of choice were shots and beer chasers. And from where I was standing, most of them looked plastered.

One of them, a man with no neck, his hair shaved, and bearing a goatee and mustache, cupped his hands over his mouth.

"Go home, cocksuckers!" he shouted, to the laughs and snorts of his compatriots.

Funny...

The tables of reporters shot him a quick glance, but quickly returned to their meals, as if they were used to his outbursts by now. Like an exhausted set of parents made to endure yet another temper tantrum from their toddler.

"So much for making friends," I said.

"Tension thick enough to shoot a bullet through it," Blood said under his breath.

To our left was a bar. There were a couple of people seated at it drinking, including one very attractive woman who was also dressed in a gray and blue law enforcement uniform.

"Maybe we should enjoy a cocktail first," I said, "while the tables and the rabble clear out. Keep the peace that way."

"Couldn't agree more," Blood said. "I hate to hurt anybody on an empty stomach."

"You like table now?" the sweet little Chinese woman said.

"We're gonna grab a drink or three if you don't mind," I said.

"Three?" she said. "You must be boozer, like prison guards."

"No," I said. "Just a figure of speech."

Her face lit up, her dark eyes wet and kind.

"Ha ha," she said. "Figure of speech...like cocksucker. That what

Correction Officer Rodney always say." She identified Rodney by
pointing her pencil at the loud-mouth, thick-necked, head shaved one.
"Cocksucker this, cocksucker that."

"Yeah," I said. "Something like that."

Together, Blood and I made our way to the bar.

CHAPTER 8

By luck or divine Providence, the bar stools that surrounded the attractive woman at the bar were unoccupied. Or maybe luck or God had nothing to do with it. Maybe it had everything to do with the fact that her uniform pegged her for the local sheriff.

Bridgette Hylton.

Since she was sitting on the ninety-degree angle at the far corner of the L-shaped bar, Blood took the seat to her right-hand side and I took the seat to her left. If I scooched to my right a little on my stool, we could all face one another.

She was drinking a Budweiser longneck. My brand. Raising my hand to snare the attention of the young man tending bar, I said, "Three Buds, please."

Blood waved his hand as if to block my order.

"Not on your life," he said. Then, "Bartender, might I inquire about your wine selection for the evening?"

The kid behind the bar was tall, impossibly thin, wearing a T-shirt that bore a black and white photo of a UK boy band called The Rixton. Printed on the back of the T-shirt were the tour dates, including one in the neighboring town of Plattsburg. He had one of those thick, round, earlobe piercings that you might see in the bush country of East Africa. His black hair was short and he wore a baseball cap over it. The cap had an extra wide flat rim and the gold sticker it'd come with was still stuck on. The hat wasn't pulled onto his head, but merely balanced upon it, cocked to one side. Ghetto style.

"Wine selection?" the kid said, while washing out a beer glass with a damp gray rag. "Why, we have an excellent Heineken, a fine Miller High Life, the classic but oh so subtle Pabst Blue Ribbon, and of course, a very rare but lovely Budweiser, two thousand and fifteen. Unless of course, you prefer a cocktail from our primo selection of generic bottom shelf booze." He swept his left hand over the shelves of no-name alcohol like gameshow host Vanna White used to do when Don Pardo belted out, "A new car!"

Sheriff Hylton burst out in laughter, until she put her hand over mouth like she'd merely coughed.

"Pardon me," she said. "Something in my throat."

For a man who rarely demeaned himself by showing any kind of emotion whatsoever, Blood looked deflated, but not defeated.

"I choose the Budweiser, young man," he said after a beat. "When in Rome."

"Dannemora is a far cry from Rome." The kid smiled. "Two Buds coming right up." Then, looking at the sheriff, "You ready?"

She picked up the bottle, glanced at what little was left. "I'll allow myself one more, since these nice gentlemen are buying."

The kid dug into the cooler, retrieved the beers, and popped the tops. He set them before us. I reached into my chest pocket on my work shirt, pulled out a twenty, set it onto the bar.

"Glass?" he said, making change.

"No, thanks," I said.

We all took sips from our beers.

Then, looking neither at me or Blood, the sheriff said, "So how much is this beer gonna cost me, Mr. Marconi and Mr. Blood?"

Blood and I exchanged glances.

"You know who we are?" he said.

Finally, she looked at Blood, then at me, smiling at us warmly.

"I'm the sheriff," she said. "As you probably are already aware. Maybe I've been completely cast aside in the search for those two on-the-lamb murderers, but I still command the respect of the governor."

"Valente called you?" I asked, recalling his ordering me to check in with Hylton as soon as I got into town.

"His assistant texted me actually," she said, picking up her iPhone from off the bar, setting it back down. "She asked me to be kind to you."

"Good of him or her," I said. "Then you know why we're here."

"Take a good look around you, Mr. Marconi," she said. "The entire joint is here for the same reason."

"True dat, Ms. Hylton," Blood said, stealing another sip of his beer, no doubt wishing it were a 2010 Malbec. "Got enough lawmen in there to start a small war."

"So you know my name too," she said, holding out her hand to Blood.

He took it in his, as if it were a delicate leaf. Her face blushed. Blood, working his magic.

She turned to me, with the same hand held out. I just shook it. No magic.

She was younger than Blood and me. Maybe just a year shy of forty. Her hair was dirty blonde, and natural. It was long enough to hug her shoulders and parted on the side neatly over her left eye. The eyes were brown and big and deep, and her lips were thick and wet from maybe one beer too many. When she smiled it wasn't out of happiness so much as out of resolve. A woman who, having gained the trust of the town of Dannemora enough to be elected sheriff, was nonetheless being told to step aside by some big-wig law enforcement agencies in the investigation to locate its two escaped cons. Something that was either going to stop her or make her more determined to go rogue and take matters into her own hands whether they liked it or not. In any case, Governor Valente was going rogue and she knew all about it. So maybe the two of them were working together. Which meant that now, she was more or less working with us.

I drank more beer, then set the bottle down onto its coaster. "So, then, Sheriff Hylton, you know why we're here and what Valente wants us to do."

"I know who he wants you to find," Hylton said, "and how, and what he wants you to do with them once you find them. That is if you can find them with all these uniforms and their hound dogs already way ahead of you."

"Where are the two cons exactly?" Blood chimed in, going for broke.

She turned to him.

"Damned if I know," she said.

"Damned if those staties know either, sheriff," he said. "Hounds or no hounds. But we got something they don't got."

"What's that, Blood?" she said.

"We got Keeper Marconi and we got me. He knows how to think like a CO and a prison supervisor. I know how to think like a criminal. We both righteous individuals. But we don't do things text book."

"That's why Valente hired you," she said.

"So you gonna help us?" I said.

"For a price, Keeper," she said.

I smirked. "How much?"

"Dinner," she said. "I'm waiting until some of those tables clear out before I can relax. That vertically challenged trooper in there sitting at the head of the table like he's Napoleon? His name is Vincent D'Amico. He's made it a personal mission in life to see that I'm entirely eliminated from the search."

"He feel threatened by you," Blood pointed out.

"He feels threatened by anyone who stands in the way of his future promotion. Including Governor Valente who likes to micro-manage things. Then there are the COs who want the staties gone ASAP."

"Can you get us inside the joint?" I posed. "Say tomorrow morning?"

"Thought you were going all Lewis and Clark," she said. "Over the river and through the woods on the trail of the bad guys."

"I need to get an idea of their level of sophistication. More than what the media's been hyping for the past sixty-plus hours. I'd like a come-to-Jesus with the warden, squeeze any info out of him I can. Preferably something that might shed some light on where they went or who, other than Joyce Mathews and Mean Gene Bender, helped them."

"You wanna speak with Joyce and Gene?" she said. "I got them both locked up in county."

"First thing after talking to the warden. All goes well, we'll be in the field no later than tomorrow afternoon."

She nodded, falling quiet.

"What is it, sheriff?" I added after a beat. "Something on your mind besides two escaped murderers?"

"The COs," she said. "They're not going to like you meddling in the case. They're very secretive about the inner workings of their prison. Their deadly sanctuary. They feel that the escape of two killers under their own watch is their business and their business only."

"That why the musclebound one with the cue ball head called us cocksuckers?" Blood said.

She pursed her lips, nodded.

"That about explains it," she said. "Baldy's name is Rodney Pappas and he's as nasty as they come. He'll do anything to defend his turf. As for D'Amico, he's playing a different game. He wants notoriety. He captures those two cons before anyone else, it will be quite the feather in his Stetson."

"What do *you* want?" Blood said.

"I want the bastards back in custody. I want this town…my town… to get back to normal. I have almost zero support staff. It's just me and a couple other bodies, and I need them here in town to keep things in order, and make sure no one takes it upon themselves to do a little convict hunting. This is wild country up here and Dannemora isn't a gun-free zone."

"Lots of people carrying guns and sidearms out there," I said. "Let me guess. Not all of them are licensed for a concealed or open carry."

She drank down her beer, ordered another round for all of us. For as attractive as she was, she was not beyond drowning her sorrows in a few beers. Couldn't say I blamed her.

"What would you suggest I do, Mr. Marconi?" she said. "Most people in this town have families. For all we know Sweet and Moss could be hiding out in somebody's attic or basement. The townspeople have a right to defend their life and limb. Defend their kids. Second Amendment says so."

"Couldn't agree more," I said.

She looked up at the kid behind the bar. He caught her gaze, smiled at her.

The old Chinese lady approached us.

"Dining room almost empty now," she said, happy-faced. She touched her mouth with her fingertips. "You wish to eat."

"There any shrimp left?" Blood said.

"Plenty shrimp," the old lady insisted.

We grabbed our beers, slid off our stools.

"Jason," Hylton said, "we're going to have dinner."

"Okay, Mom," the kid said. "Enjoy your dinner. And bring me back an egg roll."

"You got it, kid," she said.

"Mom?" I said, walking beside her back into the dining room.

"And dad too," she said. "My husband ran out years ago. Back to Buffalo. In his words, back to civilization. Jason was born when I wasn't much older than he is now."

"Tough circumstances, but looks to me like you did a hell of a parenting job. Anyone who can spar verbally with Blood has either got to be a genius or just plain crazy."

She laughed. "He's about to start his third year at Boston College. Poly sci major."

"I went to the corrections officer school of hard knocks," I said. "My graduation ceremony was the Attica riots of '71."

She says, "What about you, Keeper? Wife? Kids?"

"Never had kids," I said. "Wanted kids. But my wife died early on."

"I'm sorry."

"Long time ago. Time doesn't heal like they say it does. But it does make life more tolerable sometimes."

The dining room wasn't entirely empty it turned out. As we entered, the COs were leaving, heading for the door, the ruins left behind at their table like the dead that littered a small battlefield. The big one, Rodney Pappas…the one with the big mouth…issued us a glare that might have melted the plastic off the menus. At least he didn't spit at us.

"Rodney's the band leader," Hylton said as we sat down at the round table and took our menus from the old lady. "He's also the union rep. The one the others look up to. He hates intruders. Dannemora is his prison. From the very top to the very bottom."

"His prison broke," Blood said.

"And he knows it," she said.

"I'd like to speak with him tomorrow too, if I may, Sheriff," I said.

"Aren't you the brave one, Keeper. More than likely, he'll be the one showing us around."

"He brave all right," Blood said.

"And stupid," I said.

"Is there anything more dangerous?" Hylton said.

We all raised our beer bottles high, made a toast to bravery, stupidity, and danger.

CHAPTER 9

The next morning, we met Sheriff Hylton outside the red brick Stewarts Stop and Shop convenience store. She was standing by the glass door, already working on a large cup of coffee. When I got close to her, I could see that her face was a little pale, her eyes red and tired.

"One too many beers?" I said, not without a smile.

The punch that nailed my upper arm nearly tipped me over. Turning, I faced Blood, eyes wide.

"That how you normally address a pretty young lady first thing in the morning, Marconi?" he said. "No wonder you always lonely." Then, holding out his hand, Bridgette gently placed her hand in his. "Good morning, Ms. Hylton," he said, voice smooth and inviting. "You look ravishing, as usual."

"Why, thank you, Blood," she said, giggling. "You are such a gentleman."

He turned back to me. "Now that how you address a woman, even if she did hit the sauce a little too hard last night." He winked.

I recalled the six beers apiece we managed to polish off from the case in our motel room after we'd returned from dinner.

He who cast the first stone...

"I appreciate the collected concern, gentlemen," Hylton said. "But it's not the beers. It's the lack of sleep. Things have been a little tense around here lately."

I rolled my eyes. "Okay, thanks for the lesson in manners, Blood," I said. "But if you ever punch me before I've had my coffee again, I'll step on your big toe, and make it hurt."

"I didn't punch you," he said. "I merely tapped you to get your attention. You ain't never felt one of my punches."

He was telling the absolute truth. A Blood full-frontal-assault punch to the jaw would pretty much shatter every bone in my face. Rumor has it that during his semi-pro football days, he stiff-armed a linebacker as he was making his way to the goal line, and dented the guy's facemask. Facing the door, I made out the reflection of a van pulling up behind us, parking. A black van with tinted windows. In my head I whispered, *FBI*.

Reaching for the door handle, I pulled it open just a touch. "Can I get you anything, Ms. Hylton?"

"No, thanks, Keeper," she said. "The coffee in my hand will do the trick." I opened the door wider. "Mr. Blood, after you."

"You learning," he said as he stepped into the shop ahead of me.

Inside, the place was busy mostly with cops and troopers grabbing their morning pick-me-up. Working people in jeans and T-shirts, work boots, and soiled baseball hats. People who weren't boycotting

Starbucks, so much as they couldn't afford to shell out five bucks for a small coffee even if they wanted to. But then, Starbucks was a stranger to a strictly lower to middle class prison hamlet like Dannemora.

A uniformed trooper was standing at the counter, a cup of coffee in hand. He was staring up at the television mounted to the wall behind the cashier.

Vincent D'Amico.

I poured coffee into two large paper cups, pressed the plastic sippy lids on top, dropped a five on the counter, told the tired-looking kid working the register to keep the change.

"Thirty-six cents," he said, deadpan. "Thanks."

"I'm all about helping out my fellow man," I said.

I took a few steps back, so that I not only stood shoulder to shoulder with D'Amico, but so we both faced the flat-screen television. Rather, shoulder to shoulder was a bit of a misnomer since his shoulder only came up about as far as my elbow.

On the television, the attractive female reporter who was eating inside Fang's the night before stood outside the entry gates to Dannemora Prison. She was tall, her short dirty blonde hair parted over her right eye. Pretty eyes, ample breasts, hour-glass figure. She was speaking intensely into a handheld mic about yet another day without a clue as to the whereabouts of Moss and Sweet. That at this point, the two cons could be located anywhere from Canada to Mexico, despite the hordes of law enforcement officials having joined in the hunt. Just the sight of her provided more of a wake up than the hot caffeinated beverage in my hands.

I stole a sip of my coffee.

"Damnedest thing, isn't it?" I said, my eyes shifting from the TV to the top of D'Amico's jarhead and back again.

"What's the damnedest thing?" he said. His voice was high-pitched for an adult male, but not for a male who wasn't much taller than your average racehorse jockey. I'd always assumed the state troopers had a height requirement. Or maybe he had friends in tall places.

"The escape," I said. "You ask me, those two cons are close by."

D'Amico was an intense man. You could almost feel the tension oozing off of him, the same way you hear the buzz of high tension wires when you passed beneath them. A man ready to explode at the slightest provocation. And I felt like I just pushed one of his many buttons.

He looked up at me, quick. "I know you, chief?"

I went to hold out my right hand, politely. But then quickly realized the hand was…how do they say it in France? *Occupado.*

"Jack Marconi," I said. "My friends call me Keeper. I saw you from a distance at Fang's last night."

He nodded. "Well, Jack, what brings you to Dannemora?"

I cocked my head in the direction of the television.

"The prison break drama," I said. "But then you knew that already, didn't you?" Then, pursing my lips, "You think she's married?"

He grunted and snickered. But it wasn't a pleasant snicker.

"You a journalist?"

"Private eye," I said. "Like Mike Hammer. Only better looking."

This time he just grunted.

"Yes, the girl is married," he said. "I watch her newscast all the time. And why do you think those two escaped assholes could be close by?"

"I know prisoners," I said. "I used to be the warden at Green Haven

Prison. But that was a long time ago."

"That makes you an expert, chief?"

"More than most. Or so I'd like to think."

On the television, the broadcast shifted from the pretty journalist to a shot of the thick Adirondack forest that surrounded the prison walls. The woods looked thick, dark, foreboding. Like a place where only the Big Bad Wolf hid out.

D'Amico said, "Moss will head to Mexico first chance he gets. It's where his girl is. Where his money is. Where his home is. Depends how much Sweet holds him back."

"You think they're out of state already?"

"FBI's gonna try to pounce on this now," he said. "*Try* being the operative word here."

I shifted my gaze in the direction of the black van outside. Blood was standing by the door. He winked at me.

"I think Agents Scully and Mulder have arrived already," I said.

"The van," he said. "I saw it pull in." He watched the TV for a few beats more until Pretty Journalist came back on the screen. "So, what's your theory, chief?"

"I think they're held up in a hunting cabin somewhere. I don't think they even expected to make it out of the prison in the first place and now that they have, they're confused and scared and not sure about what their next move is. Their contact on the outside screwed them over. Their only hope of getting to Mexico now are the two living and breathing bodies that reside in the Clinton County Jail. They're desperate and hungry and sitting on their asses right under our noses. Dollars to donuts. And I'm guessing a big part of you must believe the same thing, or a version thereof anyway, or you wouldn't be devoting so much time and resources to the situation. Am I warm, Trooper D'Amico?"

"You know my name?"

"Yes, sir," I said. "I've done my homework."

"Well, chief," he said. "Do yourself a favor, and keep your nose out of official law enforcement business."

"I'm being paid to poke my nose in it. I were you, and I'm not telling you your job or anything like that, but I'd enlist a bunch of local hunters and the like. No one knows these woods better than them."

He nodded. "You mean like deputize them, create a posse comitatus?"

"Sort of. I think my boss would agree to the tactic."

"I'd ask you who your boss is, but I think I already know. And let me tell you something. You think you can come in here and undermine the work of the New York State Troopers? Well, chief, you've got yourself another thing coming."

"Whoa," I said.

He looked up at me while trying desperately not to make it look like he had to look up at me.

"What's whoa mean, chief?"

"It means you sure threw a scare into me."

On the TV, Pretty Journalist smiled. "This is Tanya Rucker reporting live from Dannemora Prison," she said. Her eyes lit up. I melted.

"You sure she's married?" I said.

"Get the hell out of here," D'Amico said.

"You asking or telling?"

He grunted again.

I found Blood standing by the door, glancing at the rack of dirty magazines.

"You just looking," I said in my best imitation Indian accent, "or are you going to buy the porno magazine?"

"I prefer the real thing," he said.

I handed the real thing his coffee and together we made a swift exit.

Outside, I eyed the black van. I couldn't see anyone inside it, but I knew they could see me. I could feel their gaze like two separate sets of red laser beams. So could Bridgette and so could Blood. The driver's side door opened on the van and a young man dressed in a dark suit stepped out. Then the passenger side door opened and a young, business-suited woman stepped out. They must have been waiting for me to re-emerge from the shop before they revealed themselves. Which told me they not only knew my ID, but knew all about my mission. Not that they'd would readily admit to anything.

"Here come the Feds," Sheriff Hylton said. "You can tell by the cheap suits."

The young man approached us, smiled. A fake smile.

"Coffee good here?" he said. His hair was cut short and trimmed professionally.

The woman stepped up behind him. Her short skirt matched her jacket. Her dark hair was pulled back in a ponytail and she wore aviator sunglasses over eyes which I imagined to be brown. "Know where we can find Sheriff Hylton?" she said. Unlike her partner, she didn't smile when she spoke. All business.

I glanced at Blood. He drank some coffee, soaking up the atmosphere, his face stoic, expressionless.

"I'm Sheriff, Hylton," Bridgette said.

"Serendipity," Blood said. The sarcasm that painted his voice was noticeable only to me. I was trained to recognize the subtleties in life.

"More like they tracked her smartphone," I said, knowing they knew exactly who the sheriff was, never mind Blood and me. But then, I guessed the cloak and dagger act was all a part of the FBI job description.

The young man pulled out his badge, flashed it.

"FBI," he said. "I'm Agent Muscolino, and this is Agent Doyle. We're here to inquire about the case of the missing prisoners."

"You don't say," Hylton said. "Thus far we have no less than four law enforcement agencies, not including the Canadian Royal Mounted Police, on the trail of those two assholes."

"What's your point?" said Doyle.

Bridgette sipped her coffee, nodded contemplatively.

"My point, Agent Doyle? Is that you will wait your turn, like the rest of us."

Muscolino went to talk, but Bridgette raised up her free hand as if to say, "Shush," immediately silencing the dark-suited spook. It wasn't easy to make out, but I was pretty sure Blood giggled.

"This is my town, agents," she said, stressing the plurality of the S on the end of agents. "That big ugly gray building behind you is my prison. Those escaped convicts are my responsibility first and foremost, and despite firm, well intentioned, but nonetheless empty promises from both Governor Valente and First Deputy Superintendent State Trooper

D'Amico, I have made it my number one goal to apprehend those two no good bastards on my own." She paused for effect. "Now, do we have ourselves an understanding, Agent Muscolino? Agent Doyle?"

They nodded, turned on their heels, got back in the van. They backed out and took off in the opposite direction of the prison gates and, apparently, a coffee shop where the atmosphere wasn't so hot.

We stood there sipping coffee and watching them disappear into the landscape. Until Blood broke the silence by saying, "You good. You very, very good, Ms. Hylton."

She smiled, proudly. "I was the first girl in this town to play Pop Warner Football. Sure, we didn't have enough boys to form a full team, but I'm the competitive type, Blood."

The coffee shop door opened. D'Amico stepped out, his coffee in hand. He stopped and stared at us, then focused his gaze on Bridgette.

"Busy catching the bad guys, Sheriff Hylton?" he said. "Or are you about to catch a hair appointment?" He cracked his lips as if attempting a wry smile brought about by his brilliant witticism, before turning and walking towards his prowler. When his boot caught on a crack in the concrete, he tripped and went down on his chest, the coffee cup hitting the concrete sidewalk and exploding all over his pristine uniform.

It was all we could do to squelch our laughs.

Slowly, he raised himself back up, while several bystanders looked on, not quite knowing what to do or how to react. He swiped at the huge brown stains that soaked his shirt and the front of his trousers. He attempted to straighten out his Stetson, which now hung off his jarhead like a bad toupee. He turned, held out his hand, pointed it at us.

"One word," he said, face full of fury. "Say even one word, or let me hear just one snicker out of your insubordinate mouths, and I will call in every statie from New York City to Buffalo and your town will be covered in the gray and black. Do I make myself clear?"

His hat slipped off his head, dropped onto the coffee covered pavement. Blood stepped forward, retrieved it for him, not before brushing away some little pieces of gravel that were stuck to the brim.

D'Amico swiped it out of his hand.

"Thank. You. Very. Much." he said, acid pouring from his mouth.

Turning, he hobbled to his prowler like a toddler with a load in his drawers, the baby-faced uniformed driver nervously opening the rear door for him.

"He very uptight," Blood said.

"That's because you and Keeper are on the job, Blood," Bridgette said. "You guys are gonna help me nail those two bastards. And soon. And he knows it."

The prowler left the scene, spitting gravel and dirt out from under its wheels. I glanced at my wristwatch.

"You think Warden Clark has shown up for work yet?" I said.

"If he's smart," Bridgette said, now walking toward her Jeep, "he'll never show up for work again."

CHAPTER 10

"**W**ill you fucking slow down? I'm starving. I ain't got the fat around the belly like you do, Picasso. I ain't got the energy stores."

Derrick Sweet is sucking air, but he's worked up enough oxygen to shout at Reginald Moss's back. A broad back covered in so much sweat, it soaks the prison green work shirt, making it appear more black than pine tree green. How ironic that Moss was worried about slowing Sweet down, when, in fact, it's worked out the opposite way. Skinny Sweet slowing doughy Moss down.

The artist trudges through the grass and thick scrub, the vegetation wet from the early morning dew that is already turning to steam in the hot sun. A heat that arrives and sticks around for only a few short weeks, but that packs the same nasty ass punch as its longer lasting winter counterpart. He's just as hungry as Sweet, just as tired, just as lonely, but what choice does he have other than to move on towards the border *regardless? It might not be Mexico, but if they can cross over to Canada, chances are they can get someone to help them get out of the country. They will have to rely on IOUs, or they might have to rob a bank or a 7-Eleven or a Chipotle Grill. Whatever. Point is, they're going to need money, a change of clothes, some hair dye, and some fake passports, just for starters.*

"Slow down, will you, Picasso?" Moss overhears as he breaks through into a clearing that seems to run for miles. He knows that just beyond the horizon is the Canadian border.

"Stop your bitching," he barks over his shoulder.

Pushing through scrub, he takes his first step into the clearing. That's when the trap springs, and the metal clamps slam closed on his shin.

CHAPTER 11

Blood took the shotgun seat while I rode in the back for the short one-mile drive to the gates of Clinton County Maximum Security Prison. We parked in the visitor's lot just like the common folk. We then made our way to a front guard shack that accessed the small visitor center, an uninviting square space that was nothing more than a glorified waiting room constructed in the 1950s or '60s. We signed in at the front desk, were handed our laminated guest badges, and told to sit tight until our escort arrived.

While we waited, we finished our coffees in relative silence, Blood having withdrawn into himself now that he was once again surrounded by four walls and some razor wire, me also choosing silence for much the same reason. There was a reason I thought twice about taking this job on. A hell of a good reason. For anyone who's ever lived or worked inside an iron house, they know how difficult it can be to make a return to the place, even if that return is voluntary and for a very limited time. Maybe you left the joint a long time ago, but the joint never leaves you. No matter how much time passes, the joint stays the same. The sickening smell wafting up from the chow hall combined with industrial disinfectant, body odor, and human piss. It is a scent that immediately sticks to the roof of your mouth and nasal passages, and it is not all that different from the smell of death. And it is just as sickening. I came close to losing my life in one of these iron houses during the Attica uprising, and even if I was just a seventeen-year-old kid right out of high school, it was something I'll never forget. Men being crucified outside their cells, men being burned alive, men with their cocks cut off and stuffed into their mouths, men shot in the head pointblank by invading state troopers. It was amazing how all those memories came flooding back just by stepping inside the prison waiting room.

Blood tossed what was left of his coffee into the trash before it came back up on him. I did the same. That was when the metal door on the opposite side of the room opened, and a man stepped through. He was a big man. Shaved head, neck the size of my thigh, clean shaven revealing a face of bumps and abrasions. A face that knew violence as much as it did human growth hormone. He was the same CO who held court at the table of COs at Fangs the previous night.

Rodney Pappas.

Bridgette stepped ahead of us, held out her hand for him. He took her hand in his, offered up a smile. Not like he wished her well. More like he wanted to fry her up, eat her for lunch.

"Bridgette, how lovely to see you again," he said, putting on his best PR song and dance. His smile was broad, his biceps squeezing out of his black work shirt. "And you brought your nice friends."

"Peter's expecting us," she said.

"And right on time," Rodney said, releasing her hand, pushing up on the utility belt that wrapped around his narrow waist and connected with the mic clipped to his shirt. "The super will be so happy to see you."

Blood and I exchanged a look, because we both knew that the last person Warden Peter Clark wanted to see right now was a member of New York State law enforcement, even if she was the town's sheriff, and someone who considered herself just as responsible for Sweet's and Moss's breakout.

Rodney looked up, gave Blood and me a glare with wide, gray eyes. He stood foursquare in his spit-polished combat boots, his black military style cargo pants tucked into them.

"You two boys ready? I'm not going to have to hold your hands now, am I?"

Blood took a step towards the door.

"You a comedian, Rodney," he said. "You missed your calling. But you refer to me as boy again, I rearrange your jaw."

"That so," Rodney said, smile tight and tense. "You never seen me in action busting some heads."

"Bet it's a sight to see," Blood said. "You must be real bad ass. How's it feel to be the bad ass chief corrections officer after Dannemora's first breakout in its century and a half history?"

Rodney's face went south fast.

"Must be he didn't break enough heads, Blood," I said.

"You two watch your mouth," Rodney said.

His smile entirely disappeared, he turned and escaped through the door into the concrete bowels of the maximum security joint. We followed. When the metal door slammed shut behind us, I felt a rock lodge itself inside my stomach. The rock told me I was trapped behind a concrete wall and inside my vile memories.

Warden Peter Clark's office was located on the second floor of the administration building. A concrete block building planted directly beside A block. The honor block that housed mostly Italian mobsters who, like Moss and Sweet, were allowed to cook their own meals with food provided by outsiders and, as it turned out, insiders. Food packages that apparently weren't always well vetted for what they might contain aside from essential nutrients, ingredients, and calories.

We entered a small front office where an attractive middle-aged woman sat behind a desk, typing something on her computer. To our right was a leather couch pressed up against the wall, and to our left, a tall green plant, the leaves of which were coated with a layer of dust.

She looked up from her work, smiled, pulled off her reading glasses, allowed them to hang off her neck by a slim gold chain.

"Can I help you?"

"They got an appointment with Clark, Betty," Rodney said.

The green-eyed woman smiled once more, fixed the bangs on her short red hair.

"But of course," she said, looking beyond Rodney's bulky build to the three of us. But, just as quickly, her eyes shifted from all of us, to one of us. Blood. "Your names, please?"

Rodney told her.

"Blood?" she said, smiling. "That's it?"

"You want my email?" he said. "Cell phone number?"

Her face went flush-pink. "Well, that won't be necessary. But if you'd like."

Blood stepped forward, wrote something down on a pink Post-it-Note from the full pad he lifted from her desk, handed it to her.

"You through playing Match dot com, Betty?" Rodney interjected. "I've got to make the headcount."

"One moment please, Rodney." Smiling, she turned, opened the door behind her, stepped inside.

Bridgette turned to Blood.

"Better watch it with that one, Blood," she said. "When she walked out on her husband five years ago, she took half his law practice with her."

"What she doing working inside a stoney lonesome, then?" he said.

"Betty likes to keep busy," the sheriff said. "Lots of nervous energy."

"Blood's type exactly," I said. "Lots of energy where it counts."

Rodney rolled his eyes, flexed his biceps. But for a brief moment, I believe Blood actually cracked a hint of a smile.

The door opened once more, and Betty announced, "Supervisor will see you now."

We went around the desk, stepped on past Betty. As though planning it that way, Blood chose to be the last one to pass her by. When he did it, he took it slow, so that she might experience his full aura, his entire uber manly being. I considered it a miracle she didn't faint on the spot.

Clark was a tall guy. Maybe six one or two. And slim. Not in-shape slim, but nervous slim. As we entered he pulled a cigarette from between his lips, punched it out in the metal dish set beside his laptop, not like he was extinguishing it, but killing it. He also closed the laptop, hard. So hard I thought he might have broken the screen.

The first thought that entered my brain: *What exactly are you hiding, Mr. Clark?*

He brushed back his thick-for-a-middle-aged-guy gray-blond hair, and fixed his blue striped rep tie so that the knot was positioned perfectly below his ample chin. I pegged his suit as a light cotton wool blend Brookes Brothers. Perfect for the summer. I couldn't make out his shoes behind the desk, but I half expected him to be wearing Gucci loafers, no socks. Like he might be hitting the beach after work instead of swatting black flies off the back of his neck outside the front door of his state-appointed Department of Corrections housing. Fancy duds for a man who brought in maybe eighty K per year, plus bennies. Who knew, maybe he'd married into some real dough.

"Terrible habit," he said, planting a polite smile on his face. "Wouldn't you agree?"

His voice came over smooth, but again, nervous. I noticed a hint of blue-blood Long Island in it. Oyster Bay maybe. Or Montauk. So what was he doing all the way out here in Little Siberia? Maybe he should have been sitting inside the corner office in a prestigious New York law firm. I almost posed the question, but then seeing how his right hand was trembling just enough for me to take notice, I decided against it.

"Smoking," I said. "Ten years quit. You never stop missing it. Totally sucks."

"I'm doomed," he said. Then, "But enough about my bad habits. Can I offer you a chair, Mr. Marconi, Sheriff Hylton, and what is it, Blood?"

Blood nodded.

"Standing is fine with me," he said, crossing his arms over his chest. He stood only inches from where Rodney stood, as if daring the big muscle-head to shove him.

Bridgette took one of the two chairs while I took the one beside hers. I crossed my legs and finger-tapped the wood arm rests. Sitting up Catholic girl-straight, Bridgette locked her hands together at the fingers.

"We're not here to interrogate you, Peter," she said, breaking the ice. "Mr. Marconi has been hired to look into Sweet's and Moss's whereabouts, and that's all."

His Adam's apple bobbed up and down in his neck. Pulling out his desk chair, he took a seat. He seemed relieved at Bridgette's comment.

"Internal Affairs down in Albany is giving me a hell of a time as you can imagine," he said, locking eyes with mine from across the length of his desk. "I understand you were once a prison supervisor, Mr. Marconi. Tell me, did anyone ever breakout under your watch?"

I nodded. "Cop killer escaped when I was overseeing Green Haven. I went after him myself. Nearly got killed in the process. The things we do to keep the iron house in order."

His face turned pale and for a moment, I thought he might cry. "I never saw it coming. I swear, I never could have imagined them getting away like they did. Cutting through the pipe, crawling through...

through…that horrible excrement."

"The cocksuckers had inside help, Mr. Clark," Rodney barked.

"Language, please," Clark said. "A lady is present." He shot Bridgette a quick, apologetic smile. "But then, I suppose you're right, Rodney. They did have inside help. However, the buck stops with me. I encouraged a lackadaisical environment. Too forgiving to my fellow man. Too easy going. Just like our President Barack Obama or Pope Francis, God bless his soul. I believed rehabilitation needed a kind hand towards some very misunderstood human beings."

"But you're not the Pope, Mr. Clark," I said. "You're a warden and they're cold blooded murderers."

He nodded, defeated.

"If you don't mind my shifting gears," I said. "You have any clue where they might have gone? If they had more help on the inside and out other than Joyce Mathews and what's his name? Mean Gene Bender."

He folded his hands atop the desk. "Not that I know of."

"Sweet and Moss confide in any other inmates about where they might hold up once they got out?"

He shook his head. "Again, no idea, and I've already told all this to the state police."

"D'Amico."

"Yes, rather unpleasant man of diminutive stature."

"I feel your pain," I said. "We had coffee with him just this morning…sort of."

I smiled. Bridgette laughed a little under her breath. Blood stood guard.

"I wish I could be of more assistance with information on where the two might have run off too," Clark went on. "But I just don't know. Or else we would have found them by now."

"Lots of woods between here and everywhere," I said. "I know D'Amico thinks they could already be on their way to Mexico, and that the Feds are about to trample on his investigation. But I'm not so sure. That would be too easy. I think they're still here somewhere and I think there's a big part of D'Amico that believes it too."

"Where's here?"

"Somewhere near Dannemora. You mind we take a look at their cell, see exactly where and what they broke out of?"

He picked up his pack of smokes, shook it so that a cigarette magically rose to the top. He popped the smoke between his lips with all the grace of a professional smoker, lit it with a silver plated Zippo not unlike the one I still owned.

"Oh, pardon me," he caught himself. "You mind? Force of habit, I suppose."

"You have an extra?" Bridgette said.

"Indeed," he said, shoving the pack towards us. I took hold of it, pulled one out, placed it between my lips. "You mind," I said holding out my hand. He placed the lighter in my palm. Flicking open the top, I lit the butt without inhaling all the way into my lungs, handed it to Bridgette. Then I set the lighter back down on the desk.

"How do you do that?" Clark said. "Don't you worry about going back? To the addiction?"

"Not at all. I vowed to quit. I'm keeping my vow."

"Such strength," he said. "Such determination. I wish I could be more like you."

He held up the cigarette in the hand that trembled. He noticed me noticing it, and he took hold of his wrist with the opposite hand.

"So whaddaya say, Mr. Clark," I said. "You gonna let us see the cell?"

He exhaled blue smoke, and stood. "It's been scoured by the state and local police. But if you must."

"Oh, we must."

He shot Rodney a glance. "Would you be so kind, Rodney?"

"I got a choice?"

Clark smiled, held out his hand. I stood up, took it in mine. The trembling hand felt small, sweaty. Frail almost. The warden might have dressed for success, but there was something very unhealthy about him. His skin showed signs of yellowing, almost like the skin on a meth addict. I'd seen it plenty of times before. A liver working overtime.

Bridgette stood up, nodded at the warden.

"Thanks for your time, Pete," she said. "I'll be in touch."

He frowned. "I suppose you will. You and IA."

That's when I heard it. Something that at first I confused for birds. Inland seagulls maybe. The kind that spend their lives flying over trash heaps. A distant and distinct, high-pitched wail. Maybe not like a bird, but more like a cat. A cat in pain, its desperate wails coming up through the old heating grates in the floor.

"You hear that?" I said to Bridgette.

"Hear what?" she said.

For a brief beat, the office fell silent.

"That," I said.

"Sounds like a cry of some kind," Blood said. As usual, his senses were more finely tuned than my own. "A woman maybe."

Clark laughed nervously. "I assure you, Mr. Blood, Mr. Marconi, there are no women presently incarcerated at the Clinton County Correctional Facility, nor have there ever been. Only hard-boiled individuals. Killers, rapists, drug dealers, confidence men, all of them."

"Sure," I said, "whatever you say, Clark. We won't waste anymore of your precious time."

He smoked, stealing such an intense drag on the cigarette, half of it turned to gray ash.

"You'd better keep that habit in check," I added. "It'll come back to haunt you."

He looked into my eyes. The look told me cigarettes were the least of his problems.

"If you don't have your health," he said. "You have nothing." But he didn't believe the cliché. Not for a second.

The four of us escaped the warden's office, no closer to finding the two cons than when we first entered.

First thing I noticed when I re-entered the reception room were the two FBI agents seated on the couch. Muscolino and Doyle. I could make out both their sets of eyes now that they weren't wearing sunglasses. Their eyes were brown.

"We meet again," I said, for lack of something wittier.

Muscolino stood. "We're close to confirming that Sweet and Moss crossed over into Canada. When it happens, you and your friend there are done. Understand?"

"What do you think, Blood?" I said. "That sounds like a stand-down threat to me."

"I don't think Agent Muscolino a very friendly guy," he said. "And we're private eyes. We don't stand down for nobody. Agent Muscolino would know that if he watched the *Rockford Files*."

"Saturday nights in the 1970's," I said. "Rockford took the nine o'clock spot in between Mary Tyler Moore and Carol Burnett."

"Let's just go," Bridgette said.

"Yeah, let's just leave the suits alone," Rodney said. At least he didn't call them cocksuckers.

I held out my hand for Muscolino. Acting on instinct, he went to shake it. But I pulled it away at the last second.

"Gotcha," I said, heading out the door.

CHAPTER 12

We waited for Blood out in the corridor while he made a solid plan with Betty for drinks later that night after work. That is, if we weren't already in the woods. In the meantime, Rodney took the time to radio the honor block, warn them of our imminent arrival.

"You're not going to find anything," he said when he was through. "Just a hole in the wall and hole in the sewer main which, if they don't patch up soon, is gonna cause a fucking riot over the stink."

Blood came back out. He was smiling. A rare occurrence for him.

"I'd ask you if you need any Cialis, Blood," I said, "but that would be like asking the Eskimos if they need extra ice."

"Pardon my hold up," Blood said. "I'm well aware we still got lots of work to do."

"We don't mind waiting around for you, Blood," Rodney said. "In fact, it's our privilege to wait around for you."

Blood looked into Rodney's eyes, unblinking. As if suddenly slapped across the face, the beefy CO turned and started down the corridor.

While we walked, Bridgette leaned into me.

"He's right, you know," she said.

"Who's right, sheriff?"

"Rodney. There won't be much to see inside the cell. I went through it myself days ago. And forgive me for saying so, because I'm the last person to tell anyone their job, but wouldn't it just be better to head out into the woods and start looking for those two jamokes that way?"

"Like I said, Bridgette, lots of territory to cover out there. Forest that's already being covered by D'Amico's staties. We go out there ill informed, we're no better than they are. Moss and Sweet no doubt hear them coming minutes before they arrive and they just find another place to hide. It's like when you try and exterminate cockroaches. They just shift to another place in the apartment. But if I can find out where their safe house is or, at the very least, a solid trail that they're following, I can catch them before they anticipate me."

"I see your logic," she said, setting her hand on my shoulder.

"I can be very logical when I want to be."

She giggled and ran her hand down my arm. Before removing it, she gently touched the back of my hand. It sent a shock up and down my spine. A very welcome touch. Maybe Blood had made a date for the night, but I was beginning to wonder if we should plan a double date.

CHAPTER 13

U nlike the other prison blocks, the honor block didn't smell of body odor and, to put it plainly, shit. The smell was more like an Italian restaurant with fresh garlic roasting on a frying pan inside one or more of the cells occupied by incarcerated wise guys. Maybe members of the Gambino family who'd been shipped to Little Siberia straight from Rikers where they'd do a third of a fifteen to twenty stretch before their private lawyers would strike up a probation deal the DA—and his or her loved ones—simply could not refuse.

The four of us climbed the stairs to the second tier of cells and walked the catwalk until we came to a cell that had been vacated by two men assigned to it. Reginald Moss and Derrick Sweet. There wasn't any plastic yellow *Do Not Enter--Crime Scene* ribbon covering the old-fashioned metal-barred cell door, but a hastily fashioned cardboard sign had been Scotch-taped to it, the words *Absolutele No Entry* penned on it in dark black Sharpie.

Blood stared at the sign.

"You bear responsibility for the homemade sign?" he said over his shoulder to Rodney.

"So what if I do?" Rodney said.

"You spelled one of the words wrong."

Rodney's roid-damaged face turned fifty shades of red.

I felt a start in my heart.

"You bustin' my balls again, right?" Rodney said. "You think I'm a dumb ass cause I'm working in a pen 'stead of on the outside, maybe for the cops."

Blood cocked his head, his eyes fixed on the cardboard sign. Clearly Rodney had self-esteem issues.

"I just pointin' out an observation, the reality of which, is a misspelled word. Accuracy means everything when it comes to law enforcement. Ain't that right, sheriff?"

Bridgette bit down on her bottom lip.

"Absolutely, Blood," she said. "*Absolutely*, with a Y, that is."

Rodney examined the cardboard sign more intently, actually positioning his eyes closer to the words.

"Absolutely…with a Y," he repeated. He stepped back. "Okay, so I fucked up. Big deal. Big fuckin' deal. Now I'm the stupid cocksucker." He drew the mic clipped to his shirt to his mouth. "Open up two-two-two," he growled.

A loud buzz shot through the cavernous concrete block building, and the barred door opened and slammed against the frame in an explosion of metal and against metal.

Rodney stepped aside.

"Make it quick, people," he said.

The three of us stepped into the cramped cell. It measured the typical six by eight feet with the metal-framed bunk beds taking up most of the wall to the right. The wall paint was hospital white that had turned gray-brown over the years and an industrial overhead lamp that spilled white light all over the concrete floor. We made our way to the back of the cell since that was where all action went down.

I faced a panel that had been painted to mimic the concrete block walls exactly. I lifted it away, exposing a hole in the wall that could easily facilitate a man. A good-sized man like Reginald Moss. Ducking my head, I made my way through the opening into a massive yet narrow pipe chase area that was dimly illuminated with red lights inside protective wall-mounted cages. Immediately I was struck by the foul odor of sewage and methane gas.

I didn't chalk up the proliferation of stink due to an old plumbing system probably originally meant to accommodate half the people housed inside this block, but instead because of the gaping hole that had been sawed out of the main line. A square hole in the half-inch thick pipe that measured a couple feet by a couple feet. Something that, like the hole in the concrete block wall, would have taken some time and commitment to create with rudimentary tools, such as old-fashioned hacksaws, chisels, and hammers. Tools the two cons purportedly utilized even if they were also rumored to have used power tools. Power tools make noise, leading me to believe that more than just one corrections officer was aware of Moss's and Sweet's intentions.

I stepped back into the cell so that the others could get a look-see.

The first to go was Bridgette, her nose clothespinned between her index finger and thumb.

"Don't light a match," I said, "or the entire place will blow."

When she came back in, Blood took his turn. In the meantime, I did some searching around the cell. Lowering myself onto all fours, I looked under the bunk beds, and in all four corners of the narrow space. I peered under the thin mattresses and pillows, pressed down on both to see if any contraband might be hidden inside them.

"Told you the joint was clean," Bridgette said, brushing back her hair, pulling it tight into a ponytail which she held in place by a rubber band.

"Trust me on this one, Bridgette," I said, "a prison cell is never clean. Take it from a former warden, there's always something left behind, no matter how small or seemingly insignificant. Something that just might give us a clue to where they landed after jumping ship."

"Keeper," Blood said from where he stood on the catwalk inside the pipe chase. "Need you to look at something."

My eyes lit up. At least I felt them light up.

"A clue after all?" the sheriff posed.

"Observe," I said.

Ducking, I went back through the rabbit hole.

Blood faced the hole. But when he raised his right arm, pointed at the fake wall panel that leaned against the bunk bed beyond the hole, I realized he was focusing on something else.

"You see the effect the red lights in the pipe chase have on that panel?" he posed.

I looked at the wash of red light on the board. He was right, something showed through the layer of gray-white paint Moss had applied to the board to make it resemble stacked concrete blocks. Repositioning myself so that one foot was planted inside the cell and the other out on the catwalk, I leaned down and stared closely at the board.

"I'll be damned," I said.

"Why?" Bridgette said.

"Lady and gentlemen," I said. "We not only have us a real clue that could lead to the whereabouts of our two escaped convicts, we have us an honest to goodness map."

CHAPTER 14

Taking hold of the lightweight balsa wood panel, I carried it with me outside the cell onto the front catwalk.

"Hey," Rodney barked, "you can't take that with you. It's police evidence."

"I'm just borrowing it," I said. Then, turning to Bridgette. "You got somebody who can scrape off this paint and reveal the map under it?"

She thought it over for a beat. "I think I have somebody in mind. Could take a little while."

"I'll use that time to speak with Joyce Mathews and Mean Gene Bender. All goes well, Blood and I will be trekking through the woods on our way to Moss's and Sweet's exact position by lunchtime."

"I prefer we go after lunch," Blood said. "And ain't you forgettin' something? Me and Betty got a date tonight."

"Sorry, old pal," I said. "You might have to raincheck with the beautiful Betty. But on the other hand, that map turns out to be solid gold, we won't even have to unpack the tent."

"I'm hoping for the latter," Blood said, pursing his lips. "I prefer civilized living."

I heard it again then. It was just as faint as it had been inside the warden's office, but still somehow unmistakable. The wail. A high-pitched noise that ran up the bony exterior of my spine and down into the nerve bundled center.

"You hear that?" I said to Blood.

He nodded.

"Must be the pipes," he said. But I sensed something else in his voice. The prison…any max security prison…was full of strange sounds that echoed throughout the steel and concrete block. Mechanical noises mostly that came from flushing toilets, humming industrial electrical fixtures, heating units that didn't work, gates opening and closing, public address systems, you name it. But this noise was different. It was animal-like. Human animal. Unexplainable and in a word, haunting.

"Could be the pipes," said Sheriff Hylton. "Or a ghost."

"There is no noise," Rodney said. "It's your imagination. Now can we be done here? I ain't got all day, people."

I felt the lightweight board in my hands. Rodney was right, much as I hated to admit it. Time was wasting. With every minute I spent researching the situation, Moss and Sweet could be gaining ground. My entire approach in their eventual apprehension depended upon their being held up in one place. Still seemed the likely scenario to me, based on my experience. And that's the reason Governor Valente had hired me in the first place. Experience.

"Show us the door, Rodney," I said.

"Gladly," he said, brushing past me on the catwalk, like I was nothing more than a stranger on the street. And an invisible one at that.

CHAPTER 15

Having packed back into Bridgette's Jeep along with the painted board from Moss's and Sweet's cell, she drove us into the heart of the town, down a couple of quiet lanes until she came to a small bungalow that, like most of the town's homes, supported a wide, screened-in front porch. What made this porch different, however, was that almost every available wall space was covered in canvases. Paintings. Landscapes mostly of the Adirondack Mountains and the surrounding forest. There were also some paintings depicting upstate lakes and rivers, and even more of some old long abandoned train stations and ramshackle houses.

Set up in the corner of the porch was an easel that supported a big canvas in the works. What looked to be an eight-point buck surrounded by lush greenery. The buck had big glassy black eyes that stared back at you when you looked into them.

Set beside the easel was something that would, under normal

circumstances, seem entirely out of place. A double-barreled shotgun.

Bridgette rang the doorbell.

"Maude," she said through the screen door. "Maude, you home?"

There was some commotion coming from the opposite side of the screen until a smallish woman with long gray, if not white, hair appeared for us in the door frame. Her face was all smiles while she held in her hands a paintbrush which she was wiping clean with a paint-stained rag.

"Bridgette, my love," she said. "To what do I owe such a pleasant surprise?"

Bridgette told her. She then introduced us.

"Come in, come in," she said, her voice and manner so affable I almost felt guilty for carrying a gun.

Standing inside the small living room, which was also covered with paintings, expect for the far wall which sported a fireplace surrounded by floor-to-ceiling bookshelves, she looked Blood and myself up and down. Rather, she focused the bulk of her attention at Blood. Go figure.

"My, my," she said, "aren't you the ruffians. Sure you're the good guys?" Giggling, she skipped into the kitchen, came back out with a plate of homemade Toll House chocolate chip cookies, which she didn't set down on the coffee table, but instead, passed around. I took two, just to be polite.

Bridgette handed her the board we nabbed from Sweet's and Moss's cell.

"Think you can get to the map underneath without ruining it? Or erasing any of the writing that might be on it?"

Maude stared at it, the same way a garage mechanic might open up the hood and examine the engine underneath. In her mind, she wasn't seeing the painted board so much as seeing what lie hidden inside it. Like she had X-ray vision.

"I'll give it a go," she said. Then, with a stern face, "But no promises."

"We'll gladly pay," I said.

"My partner on an expense account," Blood said. "Money no object."

She lightened up again. "In that case, I'll make sure to give you the premium package. But you need to give me an hour or two. Agreed?"

We all agreed.

Giving Bridgette a hug, and making sure we each took one last cookie for the road, she showed us the door.

"See you in two hours," she said through the screen door.

We piled back in the Jeep and ate our cookies.

Next stop was the county lockup, which also doubled as the sheriff's office. It was located on a country road in the town of Plattsburgh directly across the street from Sal's Pizza. When we piled out, the delicious aroma of pizza cooking in the oven immediately filled our senses.

"Who's hungry?" Blood said.

"Sal's is the best," Bridgette said, inhaling a dose of the garlic, cheese, and fresh sauce-tainted air.

"Have you noticed, Blood," I said, "that since our arrival last evening, all we've accomplished is to eat and drink our way through the Adirondacks?"

"Eating and drinking is fun," he said.

"We're supposed to be on the trail of some dangerous criminals."

"We dangerous gumshoes. But hungry gumshoes too."

"Better that we talk with Joyce and Mean Gene first, then satisfy our cravings," I said. Peering up at the sky and the black and blue clouds rapidly coming our way. "There's a storm coming," I added. "Soon as it passes, I wanna head back to Maude's, grab that map and get to the footwork portion of our program. Before Valente starts yelling at me."

"He's just the governor. He paid to yell."

There was a rumble, and the distant flash of lightning.

"Tell you what," Bridgette said. "I'll get you set up with Joyce and Gene and then order a pie for delivery to the station house."

"Righteous," Blood said. "Make it two pies."

"Righteous?" I said.

"We get some wine with that too?" Blood said.

"How about a six pack of Budweiser," said Bridgette.

"I beginning to like Dannemora," he said. "Makes me feel like a working class hero."

Several reporters and camera crews were crowded around the glass-doored entrance to the sheriff's office. Bridgette ignored their shouts for an interview as we entered into the office at the precise moment a bolt of lightning struck the road and the thunder that followed shook the building. Ominous. The thunder concussion was followed by a downpour that made the reporters scramble for cover.

The facility wasn't much to write home about. Just a small waiting area attached to an even smaller dispatch office occupied by a young dark-haired woman dressed in a deputy's uniform. She sat at a desk that had been pushed up against a reception window. A laptop computer was set on the desktop along with an old-fashioned radio and a telephone that contained several lit-up lines.

"Morning, Bridgette," she said. Then peering at her watch, "Errr, well, it's almost afternoon. Ummm, don't shoot the messenger but there's a reporter on hold on every line. You want me to get rid of them?"

"You know what to do," Bridgette said.

"Amscray with the reporters."

"We're ordering pizza, Karla," the sheriff added, stepping away from the window. "You in? Clinton County is buying."

"You betcha," Karla said from behind the window. "I'll order one pie with pepperoni and another just plain."

"Don't forget to get enough for Joyce and Gene too," Bridgette said, leading us to an interior door, the name *Bridgette Hylton, Sheriff* painted on the glass in white block letters.

We entered into the small office and faced her big wood desk while to our right-hand side was a plain wall with a bulletin board on it, to which was attached a map of the Adirondack region surrounding Dannemora. Pinned to the board beside the map were full-color 8X10s of both Reginald Moss and Derrick Sweet. Below them were photos of Mean Gene Bender and Joyce Mathews. A size-reduced printed rendering of Dannemora Prison had been pinned to the center of the map. A red circle had been drawn around A Block. A series of straight red lines extended out from the circle. The lines ran from the block following the path of the sewer line all the way to the center of Broadway, where, supposedly, the two cons escaped through a manhole cover and were supposed to meet up with their ride, Joyce Mathews.

Hollywood couldn't have scripted this one any better.

From the manhole cover, the lines spread out in three different directions. One of them ran south, as if indicating Mexico. Another ran directly into the woods to the west and stopped in the middle of nowhere, while a third and final line ran all the way up to Montreal, Canada.

Bridgette took off her sidearm, wrapped it up in the leather holster belt, set it onto her desk. She noticed me noticing the map. Taking her position directly beside me so that she, too, faced the map, she sighed.

"As you can plainly see," she said, "I'm a bit stymied."

"You would think that after three and a half days, at least a clue to their whereabouts would be found. A piece of clothing, a candy bar wrapper, something."

"People gotta eat," Blood said. "Even cons."

"Don't worry," Bridgette said. "Pizza's coming, Blood."

"You one funny sheriff."

Bridgette turned. "You wanna meet, Joyce?"

"It would be a pleasure," I said.

She went into her desk and grabbed a ring of big, heavy keys.

"Follow me to the dungeon," she said.

CHAPTER 16

His scream reverberates throughout the valley. Even the birds are so frightened they take flight from their nests. But just as quickly, Moss slaps the palm of his hand over his mouth. He knows that if someone hears the scream, their position will be compromised and the show will be over before it begins.

Overhead, the black clouds fill the sky, and already he can feel raindrops on his face. Hesitatingly, he removes the hand from his mouth, and looks down at his leg. The metal teeth that ridge the interior of the old steel trap clamps have buried themselves into his shin bone, and the skin and flesh that surround it. A piece of the shattered white bone is sticking out of the bloody, hamburger-like flesh. Just looking at it makes Moss so sick, he immediately upchucks a combination of bile and mucous.

"Oh Christ," he whispers to himself. "Get me out of here."

What he knows so far, besides the fact that his leg and his mission to get to Mexico is now totally fucked: somebody had to have planted *that antique, untagged, and very illegal trap where they did not plan on trapping a bear, like the old-time trappers used to do in the fall, but instead to catch a man. A man in the form of he and/or Sweet, to be precise. The man-poachers, whoever the fuck they are, could, in fact, be watching him right now, working up the cojones needed to pounce on his sorry ass.*

Then, coming from behind, a rustling through the thick brush.

Sweet.

The tall, skinny con stops suddenly, takes in the scene, his face assuming the expression of a man who just swallowed a live spider.

"What the fuck happened to you, Picasso?"

"What's it look like?" Moss bellows, tears in his eyes, a tremor in his voice. "I fucking stepped into a fucking bear trap. A fucking outlawed trap with fucking teeth."

Sweet feels his heart pick up speed inside his chest. His throat constricts, and his stomach grows tight. He's never seen anything like this. Not even after he ran over the cop nearly two dozen times with the pickup and the lawman's flesh resembled chewed up and spit out meat.

"What the fuck do I do?" he says, his words exiting his mouth with a tremble. "What the fuck, fuck, fuck do I do? How do I fix you, man?"

A flash of jagged lightning strikes the valley center. Thunder follows, making the earth tremble.

"Jesus, that was close," Sweet adds while peering up at the darkening sky.

"Listen to me," Moss says through clenched teeth. "You gotta open this thing up so I can free my leg."

"How you expect me to do that? I weigh a buck thirty. I've got weak arms that belong to a computer geek."

"*You gotta find a stick. A strong stick that you can use to pry it open just long enough for me to pull the leg out. Understand?*"

The rain starts coming down. Hard now.

"*Okay, okay,*" *Sweet says, his beady eyes already looking around the woods and the clearing.* "*I'll find something. Stay here.*"

"*I'm not going anywhere, dipshit.*"

Sweet doubles back, wiping the rainwater from eyes that are on the lookout for a stick. Something sturdy. Of course, the forest is full of sticks and branches. But he needs something that will fit the bill. Then, once more wiping the rain from his eyes, he sees something on the forest floor. A stick that looks sturdier than most. But also one narrow enough to fit into the small space between Picasso's mangled leg and the steel trap clamps. Grabbing the stick, he goes to Moss, takes a knee beside him.

"*Fuck, dude,*" *Sweet swallows,* "*I can hardly look at it, it's so fucking gross.*"

"*Will you just please open that trap up already?*" *Moss grouses. But he's gotta watch his mouth. The volume. It can carry, even in the woods. Even in the midst of a thunderstorm.*

"*Okay, okay,*" *Sweet says, positioning the stick in between the two cleats.* "*You ready?*"

"*Just fucking do it. Open it.*"

Sweet's seen this situation before. On old Lassie reruns. Lassie finds a dude stuck in a trap and goes for help. When she finds Timmy, she barks and trots anxiously in a circle. Timmy's just a kid, but he knows something's up.

"*What's the matter, girl?*" *he says.*

"*Bark, bark, bark,*" *says Lassie*

Timmy's eyes go wide, because he can translate those barks as easily as Han Solo can translate Chewbacca's groans and grunts.

"What's that?" Timmy says. "A man caught in a bear trap? Well, let's go save him."

"Okay, partner," Sweet says, looking down at an agonized Moss. "Here we go."

Standing, he presses both work-booted feet down on the two steel plates connected to the trap clamps. He then yanks the stick sideways, separating the clamps. The jagged teeth are yanked out of Moss's bone and flesh, the blood spurting and spraying in the falling rain. Moss screams like a girl, but somehow manages to pull his foot out from between the open clamps.

But the stick is now covered with blood and rain, making it oil-slick slippery. Physics kicks in and Sweet's left hand slides south, at the very same instant the stick snaps in two and the clamps snap shut against his thumb, severing it at the knuckle. Now it's Sweet's turn to scream while the blood spurts out of an exposed red vein. The two of them are screaming and crying and bleeding and holding to their wounds like their lives depend upon it.

"You fucking, fuck, fuck, fucking asshole, Picasso. That fucking thing took my thumb off. You fuck, fuck, fucker, I will get you for this."

"How's it my fault? Huh? How is it my fault? I'm just as fucked as you. More fucked because they're gonna have to amputate my leg if I don't get to a hospital. And right now, I can't possibly go to a hospital, never mind Mexico. You got it?"

Lightning strikes again. It's the devil's way of laughing at them. The thunder follows along with a sheet of rain. For a moment they both retreat into their pain and their misery, until a noise other than the noises associated with the forest captures their attention. It's quiet at first, but distinctive enough to raise up the hairs on the back of Moss's neck.

"You hear that, asshole?"

"What?" Sweet grouses, holding his damaged hand tightly by the wrist. "The thunder?"

"No."

"Hear what, then?"

Moss sits up, fast. "Help me up, asshole. Help. Me. Up. Now."

"Why, what's going on? What do you hear?"

"Dogs, asshole. Whoever set up that ancient hillbilly trap is coming after us with his goddamned hillbilly dogs."

CHAPTER 17

Turned out the dungeon was a cell bay that contained four concrete block spaces set side by side. The cells were accessed by a brightly lit corridor also constructed of concrete block painted hospital white, while the smooth concrete floor sported a glossy coat of industrial battleship gray with a bright yellow stripe running along the center. There were no iron barred doors in the county lockup, but instead, thick white metal doors that supported a narrow safety glass panel just left of center. Built into each door was a separate, mail-slot-like access for the exchanging of materials, meds, and food.

We stopped outside the door marked *No. 1*. I turned to Blood.

"You mind waiting out here?" I said. "Your presence might cause Joyce to faint."

"You the boss. I wouldn't want to show you up."

"You're always thinking of me."

"I don't, who will?"

As usual, Blood had a point.

Bridgette knocked on the door, shouted, "Joyce, you have a visitor!" Then, without waiting for a reply, she unlocked the door. Placing her hand on the lever-like handle set, she peered up at me. "Watch out for this one," she said. "She's a classic black window. Don't forget, she's going to be indicted for conspiracy to commit murder one with her husband as the victim. A guy who claims he still loves her no matter what."

"Now that is what I call true love," I said.

"Joyce has that effect on people. She's going to be a treat for the Grand Jury when they convene. No doubt she'll turn on the tears faucet and scream spousal abuse."

"I'm a big boy," I said, drawing my gun. "I'm trained to see through even the thickest of fogs."

"You're a big boy," Bridgette repeated. "That's precisely what Joyce is going to tell you. Then she'll try to prove it."

I smiled hungrily. "Please take good care of my 1911."

I handed her the .45, knowing that under normal circumstances, I should have checked the firearm at the front desk upon entering the facility. But Clinton County was currently engulfed in a state of emergency and SOP need not apply.

"Remember, don't do anything I wouldn't do," she said.

"I'm not easily swayed by harlots."

She made a face like, *Yeah, right*, and opened the door with all the apprehension of a mom letting her son loose on his first date.

I stepped inside and noticed immediately that the small white cell smelled of rose petals. Jail cells weren't supposed to smell that way. They were supposed to smell of rot and decay and of desperation. But this one smelled like the back room of a massage parlor. Where the high rollers went for some extra tender loving care. The walls were thick, but you could still make out the sound of rain and the rumble of the thunder emerging from out of the distance.

"Help you?" Joyce Mathews said.

She was a small, early middle-aged woman, with bleach blonde hair parted over the left eye, and the way it draped her face didn't make her appear unattractive, even to a guy like me who preferred brunettes. She was sitting on the thin stainless steel cot, her back pressed up against the wall, her white county jumper unzipped enough to expose a tight wife beater cotton T that showed off a pair of ample breasts. Tattooed on the left breast was a heart with a strand of thorns wrapped around it. The broken heart wasn't dripping blood so much as crying tears of it.

"My name is Marconi," I said. "Keeper Marconi. I'm here to ask you a few questions about the two escaped convicts."

"Keeper," she said, like a question.

"Nickname from a long time ago. Real name's Jack."

"You FBI?"

"Private investigator, so no worries."

She smiled. "Never seen one of those before, 'cept on TV."

"We exist in real life."

"Prove it."

I pulled out my wallet, showed her the laminated New York State license. She examined it, like she knew what she was examining, then looked up at me.

"Okay, I guess."

"Whew," I said, returning the wallet to my pocket. "For a second there I thought I might have to leave."

She snickered. "You're kind of a wise ass. But funny. I like funny. My husband. He wasn't funny. No sense of humor whatsoever. A man of Jesus who tolerated no sinners. Screwball if you asked me."

"You speak about him in the past tense."

"What's that mean?"

"You refer to him as something that's in the past, when, in fact, he is still alive. From what I hear anyway."

"Oh, yeah, well. If wishes were fishes…"

"…We'd all have a fry." Jeez, this woman either didn't have a clue about damning herself to death, or she harbored a serious death-by-lethal-injection wish. I added, "Your mother used to say that too?"

"My mama run out on me when I was twelve. I quit school, helped support my little brother."

"I guess you were hand-delivered a shit sandwich," I said. "I'm sorry."

"Don't be. Not your fault." She lazily allowed one of her legs to fall to the side, so that she was almost spread eagle now. I tried to ignore it. "So, what is it you want from me, Mr. Keeper Marconi?"

"Where did Moss and Sweet go after they broke out?"

"What do you mean, where'd they go?"

I sat down on the end of cot near her feet. She shifted her left leg so that her calf rested on my thigh. It sent a slight tingle throughout my nervous system that wasn't entirely unpleasant. She looked at me with her deep-set blue eyes. If I were a writer, I'd describe the look as longing.

"You were helping them out in exchange for a hit on your husband. You know exactly where they went. Now tell me, was it a secluded hunting cabin? Somewhere way off the grid?"

She brought her hand to her mouth, as if to demonstrate how shocked she was at my accusation.

"My husband wasn't perfect," she said. "And as much as I hated him, he was still my husband and I'd never thought of harming him."

"You're doing that past tense thing again."

"I am?" she said, now pressing her leg down against my thigh. "I can't imagine why I'm doing it."

"Because in your mind, he's already gone. But you reneged on your agreement to pick up the cons and they had no choice but to escape into the woods to a cabin or a safe house you know about. It was their Plan B and you know all about their Plan B, don't you?"

Slowly, she raised herself up, swung her legs around, and set her hand down on my thigh. She began inching the hand closer to another part of me that was more sensitive than the thigh.

"Do we really need to speak about those two creeps? Can't we speak about something more pleasant? Like your gun, for instance. Is it big?"

I felt her hand on my leg. "Yeah. It's big all right."

"You think you might pull it out for me sometime?"

"Maybe. But not today. Besides, another woman is holding it in her hand right now."

Now her hand was pressed on my sex. "Oh, lucky girl. I so need to feel its heaviness, its hardness. Maybe both us girls can share it. No one would know." She licked her lips. "I promise."

I had to admit, her idea wasn't entirely repulsive. Not by a long shot. Still, I was a professional after all. Keeper, the ever-in-control gumshoe. I pushed her hand aside, stood up slowly.

"You're not going to tell me anything, are you, Joyce?"

"I simply don't know anything, sweetie."

"I can help you. I know people who can help you with a reduced sentence when the DA indicts you. And you *will* be indicted and you *will* be found guilty and you *will* go back to Dannemora, or a woman's lockup just like it. But this time, you'll be residing on the opposite side of the bars."

She pouted.

"You're simply all business, Mr. Keeper sweetie," she said sadly. "Such a waste of a good man." Then, grinning, "A real *keeper*, if I don't say so myself."

"Sorry to disappoint," I said. "But I'm trying to find two escaped murderers before they succeed at murdering someone else."

The manly scream that erupted from out in the general office area was loud even inside the closed cell.

Joyce sat up at attention. "What the hell was that?"

"I think our pizza's arrived."

CHAPTER 18

I opened the door, slammed it closed behind me. I tried to pull out my .45, but it wasn't there. I sought out Blood and Bridgette. Neither were to be found. Making my way back into the main office, I saw Blood down on one knee, his 9mm semi-automatic gripped in one hand while he held onto the arm of a man who was face down on the floor with the other. Blood's knee was pressed into the small of the man's back while the man's left arm was pulled back awkwardly in a position that seemed painful and paralyzing. Set on the floor beside the man's agonized face were two pizza boxes and a black revolver. A .38 Special by the looks of it.

Bridgette stood behind Blood, her service weapon drawn. Just to the right of her, stood Karla, both her hands pressed against her mouth.

"It's Joyce's husband, Larry," she said, handing me my piece. "Looks like he came to break her out."

"Or kill her," I said, returning the .45 to the shoulder holster.

Blood grabbed Larry's other arm and pressed both his wrists together. Bridgette leaned in and cuffed him. Then Blood drew him up off the floor, stood him up. He was a dumpy man of medium height. Thick salt and pepper hair that hadn't seen a comb or a shower in ages. A pudgy face covered in stubble.

"I'm not gonna kill my Joyce," he cried. "I wanna bring her home into the arms of her loving husband and her savior, the Lord Jesus Christ."

"I admire your passion, Larry," I said. "Guns and Christ. You really thought you'd get away with it?"

"I want a lawyer," Larry said. "I don't say nothin' till I see my Joyce and a lawyer. You got that, sinners?"

"Who you callin' a sinner?" Blood said.

I swear, there were real tears falling down Larry's cheeks. If only he knew how much Joyce hated him. Outside, the reporters were salivating, their faces and cameras pressed against the glass door.

"Karla," Bridgette said. "Lock the front doors."

"Good idea," I said.

"I got another good idea," Blood said. "Leave the gun, take the pizza."

"This town is truly fucked up at the moment," Bridgette said, bringing the triangular edge of a slightly damaged piece of pizza to her mouth. She took a small bite, turning her eyes back towards the peg board and the map that was attached to it. "Why do you suppose Joyce's husband would try and spring her, knowing what he knows about her wanting to kill him?"

"Love is blind," Blood said, devouring half a slice of pepperoni in one single bite. "Christians are all about the forgiveness and the redemption. No world is so corrupt it cannot be redeemed. Less of course it's Sodom and Gomorrah, in which case, the Lord wipes the slate clean, starts all over."

"Blood's onto something," I said. "Sometimes love can be obsessive and it looks like he would have done anything to get her out, get her home, get her back into his bed and begging Jesus for forgiveness. Back to whatever they call normal. If such a thing is possible." I bit into my pizza. Bridgette was right. This was good pizza. "Question is, how did he know enough to pick up our pizza and deliver it to us?"

"He works at Sal's part time," Bridgette said. "Drive's for them, usually on weekends. Never thought to make that connection. Nor figure out that he must have picked up new hours now that Joyce was living directly across the street." Shaking her head. "Sometimes I wonder if I'm fit for this damn job."

Blood set his hand on her shoulder. "Don't be discouraged, Sheriff. Forces at work here beyond your control. Beyond anybody's control. You dig?"

"I dig," she said, her face blushing. Blood's touch had that effect on women of all ages, shapes, sizes, and creeds. Turning to me, she said, "We can head back to Maude's in a half hour. You still wanna meet Gene? See what he knows?"

I grabbed another slice of pepperoni, set it on a paper plate.

"We'll bring him lunch," I said. "Food can be a powerful motivator. Maybe it will make him talk."

"So can waterboarding," Blood said.

Gene's pizza in hand, Bridgette and I stepped out of the office and into the general booking area. A handcuffed Larry Mathews was sitting beside one of the three desks, just staring off into space while

Karla took down his vital information. It dawned on me that if he'd been able to discharge his weapon, the press and more press would have been surrounding the sheriff's office like green flies on a fresh corpse. As it was, the press was hovering over the place. But by the looks of it, Larry's Banzai scream didn't quite register with them, and that was a good thing.

"Good pizza," I said as I passed him by on my way to the cell bay.

"Sal's is the best," he said nonchalantly, as if he hadn't just burst into the sheriff's office only moment's ago brandishing a loaded hand cannon. "That's all I'm gonna say 'til my lawyer gets here. You got that, sheriff? And when do I get to see my Joyce?"

She doesn't want to see you, pal...

"You go get that lawyer, Larry," I said. "Stick it to the man, that's what I say. Even if the man, or sheriff, in this case is a beautiful woman."

Bridgette slapped my arm.

"Aren't you the charmer," she said. "I'm going to take you up on that dinner offer after all."

In the back, I found the cell marked number 4. I stood just to the left of it while Bridgette repeated the process of knocking on the metal door and shouting through it, warning Gene of a visitor. Removing my piece, I once again handed it to the sheriff. She took it, shoved the barrel into her pant waist. Unlocking the door, she opened it.

"Good luck," she said.

Pizza in hand, I stepped inside, and for the first time ever, laid naked eyes upon a naked Mean Gene Bender.

CHAPTER 19

"Gene," I said, averting my eyes. "Any chance you can put some clothes on while we talk?"

No lie. No exaggeration. He was naked as the day his mother birthed him, as if his cell doubled as a dressing hut on a nude beach in Miami. Like I anticipated, he was a big man. Cropped black hair, his skin the color of coffee ice cream, as if he were of Hispanic or Latin decent. Face clean shaven, along with the rest of his body. Other than his scalp, every bit of hair on his body was shaved or waxed or somehow eradicated from his skin. In the end I decided his skin tone was the result of a tanning booth rather than genetics. The name Bender had to be Irish, after all. Or maybe Scottish.

"Please, Gene?" I repeated. "A covering of some sort. Or no pizza."

He winked at me, smiled.

"God," he said, "can you say, homophobe?"

I guess Dannemora is definitely a prison where dropping the soap in the shower could turn out to be a major miscarriage of judgement. But then, what prison isn't?

Gene had a deep voice, but smooth in tone and, how do I put this mildly, more than a bit effeminate. Bitchy effeminate. Like my sudden presence intruded upon his aforementioned tanning booth time. Begrudgingly, he grabbed the bath towel hanging off the rack over the stainless steel toilet, wrapped it around his junk.

I immediately felt relieved, but then, maybe he was right. Maybe I was homophobic. Or maybe just plain old-fashioned and out of date, like stale white bread. Blood and I both. Or maybe I just didn't feel comfortable sharing a dead-bolted cell with a naked, body-shaved man, who was twice my size and professionally trained to protect himself against the most violent killers.

I handed him the pizza. He stared down at it, as if examining it for worms.

"The crust doesn't happen to be gluten free, does it?" he said, smirking.

"Hey, Gene, it's free of charge."

"Beggars," he said, taking a bite. "A little cold. But not bad." Then, "So, who are you, and are you the reason for all the screaming and shouting out in the booking room?"

I told him my name, my reason for being there, and that no, I wasn't the reason for the commotion. Although the woman locked up inside the same cell bay could be construed as the reason.

"Oh God," he said, his voice long and drawn out. "Larry never did have his head screwed on right. Joyce should have had him killed a long time ago." Then realizing what he said, and who he said it to, "Oopsies, I wasn't supposed to say that."

"Don't worry. I'm not the cops and our conversation is between thee and me."

"Thee and me. My, my, Mr. Marconi, you must be educated beyond your means."

He opened up his legs a little, not unlike Joyce did three cells down. Unlike Joyce, however, the maneuver didn't turn me on in the least. He ate more pizza. Or, should I say, nibbled.

"Listen," I said, "I'm gonna get right to it. I'm not interested in why you helped Sweet and Moss, or how much you helped them and for how long. What I'm interested in is where exactly did they go after they escaped?"

"How should I know?" he said, his eyed focused not on me, but at the plain white wall across from him. Dollars to donuts, he wasn't looking at the wall though, but instead, Reginald Moss.

"From what I heard, you and Moss had yourselves...how shall I put this delicately...a rather personal, if not intimate relationship."

He cocked his head. "Reginald liked to paint me pictures. His artwork is incredible. Such a sensitive, tortured, helpless, misunderstood artist."

"And in return..."

"And in return I'd bring him gifts. Food, booze, new CD recordings of my band, grass sometimes, stuff like that."

"And..."

His face turned red. Maybe I'd only just met him. But if I didn't know any better, I'd say Mean Gene Bender had real feelings for Reginald Moss, escaped killer.

"And?" he repeated. "I really have to say it?"

"You don't have to say anything, since we already know the nature of your relationship with the escapee."

"Okay, you ready for this? I used to suck him off. He has a huge cock. Bigger than yours certainly."

I looked down at my lap. "It's not the length that counts."

"Yes, it is," he said. "Take it from one who knoweth."

"Now that we have *that* established, I'm guessing Reginald told you precisely his plans. Where he'd rendezvous once he killed off Joyce's husband, Larry." Pressing my lips together, cocking my head. "You know, pillow talk stuff."

He took another small bite of pizza, made a sour face, and tossed what was left into the wall-mounted trash receptacle.

"You don't like Sal's?" I said.

"It doesn't like my waist."

He was muscular. Cut even. Veiny wiry. He obviously took pride in his appearance. The way he appeared naked. The way he appeared playing bass in his band on stage in some crappy biker bar. Or so I imagined.

"Tell you what, Mr. Marconi," he said. "First of all, I don't know shit. But if I did know some shit, what do I get out of revealing it to you?"

I had to think quick. I really had nothing to offer him. I wasn't a real cop, or a lawyer. I wasn't a real anything other than a PI. A PI who really missed his wife, Fran, even nineteen years after the hit and run that snuffed out her life. This too was real: I was working for the governor. Maybe I could use that relationship to my advantage.

"What if I were to tell you I could see about getting you a reduced sentence?"

"Everybody offers that. You watch too much TV. *CSI Miami*."

"More like *Miami Vice* reruns," I said. "I'm still living in the 1970s and '80s."

"You're dating yourself."

"Whatever. But I mean it when I say I can go to bat for you. Can't promise the outcome. I can, however, try. But you gotta give me something first."

He sighed.

"What the fuck," he said. "I'm in jail, so what difference does it make at this point?" He resumed staring at the white wall. A wall that no doubt bore the face of Reginald Moss and maybe even Derrick Sweet. "Moss wanted to go to Mexico," he said after a beat.

"I know that already. But it's not like he could just head to the airport, hop a Southwest flight direct to Mexico City."

He nodded. "The two of them needed a place to hide while things calmed down. A place no one would find them, at least in the first few days. No one other than Joyce, that is, who never showed up."

"Let me guess. A hunting cabin. In the deep woods. Something off the grid. Maybe with a basement."

"You know your stuff."

"Where, exactly?"

Another sigh. More like an exaggerated exhale.

"There's an old railroad bed to the west of the prison and the town. Been out of service for years and years. You follow that for a couple of miles. There's some kind of marker that indicates a turn-off. Joyce Mathews placed a marker there."

"What kind of marker?"

"I have no clue. But, apparently, Moss and Sweet would know it when they came to it. They were to turn off there, bushwhack into the woods heading north at ninety degrees for another mile. Eventually, they'd come upon the shelter. They'd wait for Joyce there."

"Shelter?"

"Not a cabin necessarily, but something dug out of the forest floor. Constructed by some survivalist freak back in the 1950s. Somebody convinced the Russians were gonna invade, drop the bomb, whatever."

"No wonder D'Amico's been striking out."

"That guy's a major dick."

"Couldn't agree more. But he's got a job to do."

"So," he says, sitting up, placing his hand on my thigh, "how do I know you're going to uphold your end of the bargain? Get me a reduced sentence?"

I took a step back so that his hand fell off.

"You don't," I said. "You're just gonna have to trust me."

"Trust," he said, "what's that?"

"It's like faith. You can't see it or feel it or touch it. You just have to believe in it."

He smiled sadly, opened his mouth as if to say something, but then decided against it. At that point, I sensed he truly missed Reginald Moss and that he knew he might never have the chance to see him again. Maybe that was why he was so willing to reveal the hideout. Maybe he felt that by opening up to me, instead of the police, Moss might have a real chance at being caught and surviving. Of course, his motivation might lie elsewhere. For instance, the life expectancy for a former screw incarcerated inside a maximum security joint was maybe two weeks. That is, management didn't decide to lock him up in the box twenty-four seven, which was its own form of slow death.

I turned for the door, but then turned back.

"Can I ask you something?" I said.

"You're standing there, aren't you?"

"Why do they call you Mean Gene? I'm not seeing anything mean about you at all."

He laughed under his breath. "It's a nickname Reginald came up with. I guess he didn't want anyone messing with me. So he called me, Mean Gene. Don't mess with Mean Gene. Mean Gene will knock your block off, you touch him." He looked up at me from down on his side on the hard-as-a-rock cot. "You see, Mr. Marconi. Moss wanted me all to himself."

I wondered if he was aware that Moss had also been bedding down blonde bombshell, Joyce. But I decided not to press him on the issue. I just didn't see the point.

Turning back to the door, I wrapped on it with my knuckles. The bone against metal told Bridgette I wanted out.

She stood outside the cell, staring into her smartphone.

"Looks like Maude is pulling through for us. She sent these over ten minutes ago," she said, holding up her phone so I could clearly see the screen. The photo showed a map, parts of which were still stained by patches of gray paint, but I could also clearly make out lines that had been drawn on it, perhaps indicating the precise location of the shelter Mean Gene had been talking about.

"Can you enlarge it for me?" She touched the screen, making the picture bigger. But a bigger picture meant a serious lack of focus, so that making out anything proved even harder. We'd have to see the real thing for ourselves.

"Where's Blood, Sheriff?"

"Sleeping off the pizza in my office."

"Let's wake him up and get back over to Maude's. That map, taken with what Mean Gene just confessed, might give us something that no other law professional on earth has right now."

"What's that, Keeper?"

"The precise location of those two escaped cons."

CHAPTER 20

When I tapped Blood on the shoulder, he slowly sat up.

"Just resting my eyes is all, Keep."

I told him we were going back to Maude's, now. Then, we enter the woods.

"I hope she made more cookies," he said.

"We'll take some for the hike."

Bridgette grabbed her Jeep keys.

"Vamoose, muchachos," she said.

"Hasta la vista…baby," I said in my best imitation Arnold.

Blood laughed. Not with me. But at me.

Nothing looked out of place when Bridgette pulled up to Maude's bungalow. We slipped out of the Jeep, made our way up the front steps and onto the porch. When I looked over my shoulder at the easel set up at the far end of the room, I noticed something was missing.

The shotgun.

"Something's not right," I said to Bridgette.

She looked up at me wide-eyed, then opened the door, stepped inside.

"Maude!" she barked.

Blood pulled out his gun. I did the same. So did Bridgette.

"I'll get the back," Blood said, about-facing, heading back down the porch steps.

"Maude, honey, you here?" Bridgette shouted once more.

"I'll take upstairs," I said, entering. "You be careful, sheriff."

I bounded up the wood stairs two at a time. Coming to the landing, I scanned the hallway with the barrel on the .45, like it was a tank turret. I went right, checked the small bathroom, threw open the shower curtain. The tub was empty. I crossed the hall, checked out the first bedroom. It, too, was empty.

That was when I heard something I didn't want to hear coming from downstairs. A gut wrenching scream.

"Good Christ, Maude!" Bridgette yelled. "What the hell did those bastards do to you?"

Heading back down the stairs, I entered into the kitchen at precisely the same time Blood did. As soon as my boot soles met the old yellow linoleum, I saw the feet that belonged to a body laid out in the back pantry section of the kitchen. The double-barreled shotgun was also lying on the floor beside her. That the leather sandaled feet belonged to Maude, I had no doubt. This gentle woman gave us cookies just a short two hours ago. A sweet gesture that made her violent homicide seem all the more wrong. I almost didn't want to look. But how could I not look?

Bridgette turned away, wiped a tear from her eye, stepped into the adjoining dining room. Together, Blood and I stood over the body. Not only had her neck been sliced from ear to ear, whoever slaughtered her thought it prudent to jam the cone-shaped paint brush handle through her left eye. Taking a knee, I picked up the shotgun, cracked open the breach. The shells were still live. She never got a shot off.

"That thing in her eye," Blood said after a long, sad beat. "It take some strength to do that shit."

"And a black heart," I said. Then, standing, "The map. Anyone seen the map?"

A drafting table occupied the far corner of the dining room. A draftsman's lamp clamped to the table was still lit up, indicating that Maude had been using it when whoever killed her intruded. I went to the table, saw that it had been ransacked. Paper towels soaked in gray paint and paint remover littered the table surface and the paint-stained wood floor.

"This is where she worked on the board," I said. "Whoever killed her took it."

"I'll check upstairs just to make sure," Bridgette said.

She ran up the stairs while Blood and I made a futile check of the downstairs and even the basement. Back in the kitchen, Bridgette shook her head.

"No board," she said. "Whoever did this didn't want us to get at that map."

My mind spun like a wheel of fortune until it stopped on a clear vision of Rodney standing outside the prison cell.

"Rodney was the only one who knew we took the board," I said.

Bridgette went for her chest-mounted radio, like she was about to call the murder in.

"Wait," I said. "Not yet. We bust Rodney now it's just our word against his. Plus, I'm beginning to think there's something more to this than just two cons who wanted to jump the walls of this prison."

The wailing...the crying...the high-pitched voices rising up from within...

"Me too," Blood said. "There something going on inside that prison. Something bad. I can feel it."

"Listen, Bridgette," I said, "you take in Rodney now, they'll whitewash whatever it is they have going on somewhere in the depths of that place."

"Maude was my godmother, Keeper," she said, her eyes wet, her face pale with sadness.

"I know how you feel," I said. "But our best bet is to cut to the chase, go after Moss and Sweet now that we have at least some idea of where they are. While D'Amico is still in the dark and the FBI are operating outside their jurisdiction."

"In other words, sheriff," Blood said, "what Keeper's trying to say is, let's go get them two fucks while we still have at least some control of a situation that is clearly going south fast."

Her eyes went wide. "You think Clark and Rodney and the two cons are in on this together, don't you?"

In my head, I once more heard the faint but high-pitched, almost screaming voices coming from the depths of the prison.

"Joyce and Mean Gene were in on it. Who knows the extent of what's happening inside the iron house?"

"But what will you do now that there's no map?" Bridgette said.

It dawned on me then. "You showed me a cell phone pic of the map just a few minutes ago. Maybe if Maude's phone is still lying around, we'll find even more pictures of the map on it."

"Question is," Bridgette said, "where's her phone?"

"The most obvious place," I said.

"Read you loud and clear, boss man," Blood said.

He went back into the kitchen, turned into the pantry. Bending at the knees, he started going through the pockets of Maude's baggy jeans. He came back out with a smartphone. Even from out in the dining room, I could see that it was an Android packed inside a red and white protective case. When Blood turned the phone over, we could make out the big words printed on the case back.

Art Slut.

"Whoever did this to her didn't think of looking for her phone," Blood said. "They must have been in a panic, or amateurs, or both."

We all gathered a few steps away inside the kitchen and Blood handed the phone to Bridgette.

"You know the code that unlock the screen?" he said.

Bridgette bit down on her bottom lip. "I can try. Her birthday would be a good start."

She punched in the digits.

"It's no good," she said. "We have, at most, nine more tries before the phone locks us out for good. Ideas?"

My eyes focused on the protective cover.

"How about art slut?"

"Worth a shot," Bridgette said.

She typed it in. The phone unlocked.

All three of us anxiously stared at the screen while she used the pad of her index finger to access the gallery and the most recent pictures. The first, and what I could only assume was the last photo snapped before her murder, showed a blurry if not distorted image of what appeared to be two men. Their torsos actually. One dressed in black, the other in blue. They seem to be approaching her from the direction of the living room.

"Recognize these people?" I said.

Bridgette shook her head.

"It's impossible," she said. "The picture is so distorted and no faces."

I held out my hand.

"May I?" I said.

I enlarged the picture, stared down at it for a few beats. There were definitely two people…men…in the foreground, and even the possibility of someone in the background. A third person. I thought about making my observation known to all, but my gut told me to shut up about it. Right now, the important things were the map's and the con's location.

I shuffled to the next picture. The map. It wasn't the picture that Maude had sent to Bridgette while we were in the Sheriff's office. It was a better picture. One she'd probably taken after the one she'd sent. I enlarged it. A series of lines led through the forest west of the prison, not far from the rail bed that Gene had spoken about. There was an X drawn in red Sharpie that, in my mind at least, indicated precisely the spot in which we would find Reginald Moss and Derrick Sweet. If they were still hold up. And knowing that the state police were out en force, and now with a posse of hunters and their dogs, it made sense that they would be.

"You see that, people?" I said. "You see that red X?"

"X marks the spot," Blood said.

I pocketed the phone. "Bridgette, I assume you need to call in the proper authorities to take care of Maude's body? Maybe even the state police? Plattsburgh CSI?"

"I'm already on it. I'm staring down the barrel of a homicide that's directly related to the prison break."

"Blood and I are heading for the woods. I'll radio you for backup when our mission is accomplished."

She nodded. "You'll need a ride back to your Toyota."

"It's four blocks," I said. "We'll take it double time."

She showed us to the door. I opened it for Blood. He stepped out and started making his way down towards the road. I went to step out. But Bridgette grabbed my jacket sleeve. She leaned into me, kissed me on the cheek. Lovingly.

"Be careful," she said. "Those men are killers."

"So am I," I said. Then I leaned in, kissed her on the mouth.

On the quick walk back to the motel, a black van pulled up.

The black van. The FBI.

We stopped. The window on the passenger side came down.

"Where you off to in such a rush?" said Agent Muscolino from behind the wheel.

"I gotta pee," I said.

"Me too," Blood said. "Too much coffee this morning."

"Anything to report on behalf of the ongoing quest for our missing cons?"

I stared into Muscolino's sunglass-covered eyes, and then into his partner's eyes. They were like emotionless robots.

"Not a thing," I said. "But rest assured, when we do, you fine federales will be the first to know."

"That's reassuring," Muscolino said. "In the meantime, we've called in reinforcements. By tonight, this investigation will officially be in the hands of the Federal Bureau of Investigation."

"I've got chills," I said.

"Me too," said Blood. "You got any extra FBI T-shirts in the van? Size extra-large? Maybe a couple Agent Muscolino and Agent Doyle bobble-head dolls?"

Muscolino pressed his thins lips together, sneered at us, thumbed the window up, and pulled away.

"They takin' over," Blood said. "They do that, you get fired, lose out on your pay."

"They take over, this thing is gonna end in a blood bath. I've seen it happen before when the Feds take charge."

"Could end in a blood bath anyway. Maude's lying dead on her own pantry floor. We should have let Muscolino know about it."

"He'll find out soon enough."

"Maybe he already know."

"One thing's for sure," I said.

"What's that?"

"We need to find those two cop killing assholes. Find them now. Before anyone else dies."

CHAPTER 21

Back at the motel, Blood and I prepped for battle. Both of us changed out of our street clothes and into black fatigues and matching T-shirts, our equipment stuffed windbreakers over that. We carried our sidearms in shoulder holsters, and we carried additional magazines in holders strapped to our belts. While we painted our faces with black camo, we finished the last few beers and watched a live news report on the wall-mounted high-def television.

A stunning Tanya Rucker stood in front of the prison gates, her mic held steadily just beneath cleavage revealed by a light blue, silk button-down blouse.

"The manhunt continues for two escaped murderers in the thick Adirondack forest while the small town of Dannemora remains on lockdown. With numerous law enforcement agencies continuing their vigilant, yet as of this moment, futile search for Reginald Moss and Derrick Sweet—a search personally spearheaded by the New York

State Troopers and in particular, Trooper First Deputy Superintendent Vincent D'Amico—little in the way of progress has been made in the nearly four days since the convicts managed their daring, Hollywood-like escape. Moments ago, I spoke with D'Amico about his plans for upping his game against the convicts."

The broadcast shifted to a taped shot of D'Amico standing in an open field located by the side of the road. Opposite the road were the woods. There were several hunters standing on the shoulder of the road. They were dressed in camo, hunting rifles slung to their shoulders, several varieties of hunting dogs obediently standing or sitting by their side. It looked like a deer hunt about to commence in the middle of the summer.

The lovely Tanya asked D'Amico why he felt it necessary to enlist the help of the local hunting population in the apprehension of the dangerous criminals especially when his support staff should be, in theory at least, so well trained in the art of criminal capture.

"The deep woods are a different animal than say a suburb or an urban environment," he said, face stern, the brim on his gray Stetson pulled far down on his forehead, like he practiced the look in the mirror prior to the interview. "No one knows them like the local boys. They know every tree, every branch, every rock under which two snakes like Moss and Sweet can hide. It only makes sense we employ these fine men and women. It also makes sense to offer a substantial one hundred thousand dollar reward for the capture of said snakes, dead or alive. It's common practice for soldiers to hire local scouts for the capture of hard-to-uncover enemy soldiers during wartime. And trust me, this is war."

He nodded, touched the brim of his hat like he were a diminutive Clint Eastwood in *The Good, The Bad and the Ugly*, and walked away into the sun. The broadcast then switched back to the present and the journalist whose eyes peered directly into the camera. Peering directly at me. Or perhaps that was just wishful thinking.

"So what originally had been called a search that would end within twenty-four hours by our own governor, now drags on towards its fourth day. It remains to be seen if deputizing the local talent can prove the final remedy for curing this dangerous and volatile situation in and around the small but shocked upstate New York town of Dannemora. But for now, it seems the *only* remedy worth pursuing. This is Tanya Rucker reporting live from the Clinton County Correctional Facility for Fox News 13."

"She's married," I said while I picked up the clicker and turned the television off.

"She not your type anyway," Blood said. "She good looking and smart." He crushed his now empty beer can in his hubcap-sized hand, made a three-point toss from the opposite side of the room to the metal waste basket situated beside the desk. A perfect toss. "Score," he said. "All net, baby."

"Val wouldn't like hearing you say that." I consumed the rest of my beer, crushed the can, tossed it at the waste basket from a distance of five feet away, and whiffed miserably. "Why do I feel really white right now?" I whispered.

"You right," Blood went on. "Val is the exception. She a brown-eyed, long brunette-haired beauty, and she smart too. Which means it be about time you married her, you dope."

He spoke the truth, naturally. But I would never admit to it. Keeper, the lonely and the stubborn.

"You know what happens when you get married, Blood?" I said, capping the camo tin, placing it back inside my bag.

"No, what happens when you commit to someone who loves you without condition?" he said, capping his own camo tin, placing it into his own satchel. FYI: didn't matter that Blood was dark-skinned. A healthy dose of camo provided him with even more stealth than he was born with.

"Someone always gets hurt," I said. "Someone's always got to die first. Or get sick first. Or sick and tired. And I already been through that shit."

"It's a long life that's getting shorter by the minute," he said. "You should share it with someone who cares. Val loves you. Don't know why, but she does. You should stop being selfish and buy her a ring."

"You gotta be seeing one another for that to happen, and right now we're not seeing one another."

I lifted the AR-15 from off the bed, released the magazine, checked to make sure the .223 rounds were packed inside the illegal twenty-round mag the right way so that the piece wouldn't jam at the wrong time. Not that there was ever a right time. Then I punched the magazine into the breach, cocked back the slide that forced a round into the chamber. Safety on, I placed the rifle strap around my shoulder, put on my skull cap, and then slipped my black ballistic gloves on my hands. The time to go hunting had arrived.

"Now," I said, "can we go before I tear up over all this love-gone-horribly-wrong talk?"

Blood grabbed hold of his AR-15, pulled back the slide, thumbed the safety on.

"Love stinks, Keeper," he said. "But love is also a many splendored thing."

CHAPTER 22

By the time they make it back to the bunker entry, they've left a blood trail that should be ripe sniffings for some bounty hungry redneck's hunting dog. One of those great big black labs that drools all over your hand, or a hound that can't stop marking his territory with a thick, hot, steaming, nuclear yellow stream of dog piss. So thinks a suffering Reginald Moss, while a one-handed Derrick Sweet removes the brush that hid the metal silo-like tower from prying eyes.

"You gonna fuckin' help me with this thing, Picasso? Or you gonna make me do all the dirty work while you sit there and bleed?"

"My fucking leg is shattered. I've suffered a compound fracture. What exactly is it you'd like me to do, asshole?"

"Your fucking leg is shattered? That's it? That's all you got to bitch about?" Holding out his injured hand. "My fucking thumb got cut off. It's gone. That hand ain't never gonna be right now."

Moss laughs. "So now you're gonna have to jerk off with your other hand. But it's okay 'cause it feels like another woman."

"Fuck you, Picasso. I should have taken off when I could. I'd be in Mexico by now, sitting on the beach with two healthy thumbs, one of them shoved up the ass of an eighteen-year-old brunette, brown-eyed, grande tetted senorita. But you just had to wait around for a couple of days until the coast was clear. You had to play it safe, and I was the stupid jerk who listened."

"You forget our contacts on the outside abandoned us. We got no choice but to hold up."

Sweet unlocks the padlock, lifts up on the latch on the square metal panel door with his good hand, pulls it open. There's a metal ladder attached to the concrete wall that leads down into the shelter space.

"Think you can make the decent down into the shelter, Picasso? 'Cause Lord knows I can't carry your heavy ass."

"No. Fucking. Choice," Moss grumbles.

The big man shifts himself on his ass until he's directly beside the opening, maneuvers his mangled leg into the round shaft and, at the same time, lets loose with a painful howl that must pierce the ears of every canine within a ten-mile radius. He sticks his good foot onto the fifth ladder rung down, while grabbing hold of the cylindrical metal shelter frame with both his hands. In that manner—working with his three operational limbs—he makes his way slowly down into the shelter, knowing with each inch descended, he is never going to see the light of day again. He might as well be cutting to the chase and entering hell while his heart still beats.

Sweet is also down to three workable limbs. He enters into the shaft and manages to close the lid behind him, while padlocking it from the inside. Does it by wrapping his bad arm around the top vertical ladder rung. *The shelter secured, he makes his way down into the interior, his freedom-starved brain hungry for visions of a white-sanded Mexican beach, a topless tart on his arm, a perspiring bottle of Corona set on a wood table beside a mirror sweetened with half a dozen primo lines of El Chapo love powder.*

Both injured men spend the next few minutes fixing up their separate wounds as best they can with the first aid and medical supplies at hand. Moss applies a splint to his leg, wraps it tight with gauze and medical tape. He even locates a pair of crutches in one of the closets. Sweet does his best to stem the bleeding from his wound by applying two small butterfly clamps to the stub of a thumb, and then wrapping it with gauze and half a roll of white surgical tape. Although no one comes out and says it, both cons know deep down that if they don't get proper medical treatment soon, they face gangrene and death, possibly within seventy-two hours. But they choose not to talk about this. Better to live like old age is still a real possibility for them.

When the patching up is finally finished, Sweet faces his partner.

"So what now?" he says. "We stay here until the food runs out and we got no choice but to eat each other?"

"We need to gear up. Gather weapons and ammo, just like that last stand on the bridge in Private Ryan," Moss says. He hobbles to the table set in the center of the room. "Somebody's gonna come for us, and when they do, it ain't gonna be pretty."

"How they gonna get to us? It's a bomb shelter. We're locked inside this underground tin can."

"Trust me, they'll find a way in. And when they do, we're gonna have to shoot our way out of it or die."

Sweet shakes his head, goes to the cabinet on the far wall, opens it.

That's where he finds the two riot shotguns, plus two M16s, several varieties of sidearms and at least a thousand rounds of two or three different calibers. He starts with shotguns, handing one of them off to Moss. He then hands off an M16 and a 9mm sidearm to go with the one he was already packing when they walked away from the shelter earlier, thinking they'd never have to step back inside it again. He distributes the ammo and the various magazines. For a time they sit there, wounds throbbing, contemplating the empty magazines. Until Moss begins loading the first magazine while the one-handed Sweet looks on in relative silence. When everything is locked and loaded, they sit there listening to one another breathing. Hating one another. Wishing one another dead.

"Got any cigarettes left?" Moss says.

"Smoked the last one this morning. Didn't think we'd be coming back here."

Moss nods, his heart beating in time to the throbbing in his foot and leg. When the sound of a boot sole pouncing on top of the metal hatch reverberates throughout the underground shelter, Moss grabs hold of the shotgun, pumps the action, forcing a shell into the chamber.

"This is it," he says, swallowing. "This is where the Germans take the bridge, kill Tom Hanks and poor misunderstood Tommy Sizemore. The fucking Nazis kill us all."

That's when Sweet runs to the toilet and pukes.

CHAPTER 23

We parked my Toyota 4Runner in a patch of woods only a few feet from the old abandoned rail bed. I made sure to park it behind some thick brush so that D'Amico's men might miss it altogether should they pass it by. But I also made sure that it wasn't parked all that far from where I felt fairly certain we would find the two fugitives. We would need it for transporting them back up to Albany and to my employer's doorstep at the Governor's Mansion on Eagle Street. The less distance required to drag them through the woods, the better.

The rail bed was overgrown with weeds and brush. Some of the railroad ties were either missing or rotted out. The rails were rusty in spots and, on occasion, non-existent, as if somebody hack-sawed a five-foot section here, a three-foot section there, for their own use to sell off for scrap. We walked swiftly, but not so fast we'd miss the marker that Joyce Mathews placed conspicuously for the two cons. Whatever that marker turned out to be. Gene said Sweet and Moss would recognize it when they came to it, so why shouldn't we recognize it too? But that might be wishful thinking.

We carried the AR-15s rather than utilize the shoulder straps, like we were on patrol in Viet Nam or Afghanistan, not saying anything, not needing to speak, needing instead to concentrate on the task at hand, knowing that at any moment a vigilant Moss and Sweet could ambush us. A not too far-fetched situation considering the desperation the two men must have felt by then.

A couple more minutes passed before I spotted the red kerchief tied to the tree branch. Raising up my right hand to signal stop, I faced the old oak tree.

"Whaddaya think, Blood?" I said, voice low, tone soft.

"Look like a marker to me," he said. "But then, what do I know?"

"What does your gut say?"

"Half my gut say D'Amico and his men passed by this very rag a hundred and one times already," he said. "But the other half of my gut says D'Amico got his head up his ass and that's the marker we looking for. That what the gut say."

"Mine too."

I pulled out Maude's smartphone, typed in *art slut* in the area required, and then went to the picture gallery. I found the map that contained the X and tried to get my bearings. Enlarging the photo, I held the phone in the palm of my hand so that Blood could get a good look also.

"That's the railroad bed," I said. Tapping the picture with my index finger. "I'd say we're standing right about here."

He nodded. "If you right, we only a couple hundred feet away from where X marks the spot."

"Safeties off," I said, thumbing the safety into its vertical firing position.

"Safeties off," Blood repeated.

We stepped into the woods, and with the semi-automatic rifle barrels aimed for whatever might come our way, we proceeded to punch our way through the thick brush, step by careful step. It was slow going at first, but eventually the woods thinned out. A few long beats passed before we broke through the brush entirely and came upon a small clearing that measured maybe ten feet by ten feet.

Blood and I stopped in our tracks.

Positioned on the forest floor before us was a cylindrical solid metal door that led to some sort of underground space. And standing atop the metal door, his rifle barrel staring us in our respective faces, was a hunter and his dog.

CHAPTER 24

Turned out, the hunter didn't hunt alone. Emerging from the thick patch of woods behind him, a second hunter stared us down with the business end of his rifle.

"You," said the first hunter, "drop your weapons."

"You asking or telling?" I said, my pulse pounding in my temples, mouth dry.

He was a short man sporting a round beer gut that looked like he'd swallowed a basketball. Middle aged. Dressed in camo from head to toe. His dog, a hound, was standing foursquare, just a hint of growl boiling from behind its white teeth. I knew all it would take was a simple, "Sic 'em," and the pooch would be on me in a New York millisecond. Hunter number two was taller, thinner, also sporting camo. He had a cancer beard that immediately reminded me of a character out of the 1970s classic film *Deliverance*.

"You heard the man," he said, his voice high-pitched and nervous.

"Drop your weapon. Same goes for the spook."

The dreaded S word.

I considered Blood a man of calm and coolness. Therein lie his beauty. He was also a man of great principle and moral aptitude. I knew that the use of the S word would spark something in him that, if left to fester, would cause him to explode. And that explosion would not be a good thing for these two local yokels.

"I'm going to say this once," I said, shouldering my AR-15. "First of all, we both want the same thing. The capture of those two cons. Second, if you use a disparaging term like that once more, I will shoot you both in the face and gladly face the consequences later. Am I understood?"

Short Beer Gut began to tremble now. He was obviously way in over his head.

"You just wanna take our reward money," he said. "That money is ours. We ain't got jobs and we aims to take it all."

Tall Cancer Beard drew back the bolt on his weapon, then pushed it forward. A single deadly round now locked and loaded.

"What we have here," he said in an anxious high-pitched voice, "is a Mexically stand-off. Only with a spook and his white, creamy assed, butt buddy." He spit some black tobacco juice and shifted the index finger on his shooting hand inside the trigger guard so that it rested on the trigger.

That was when Blood took off for the woods, as swiftly as a mountain lion seeking out its prey.

The two men turned their heads, one way and then the other. They never expected Blood to run like that. Never expected anything but the upper hand.

"Where'd he go?" barked Tall Cancer Beard. "Where'd the spook run off to?"

"How the hell do I know? I got my hands full with this one." Then, his Adam's apple bobbing up and down in his throat, "Say, you two ain't cops, are you? We never thought to ask them if they's cops."

Tall Cancer Beard opened his mouth as if to speak, but before he could get a word out, Blood burst through the woods on the opposite side of the clearing, fighting knife gripped in his hand.

CHAPTER 25

Eight-inch titanium blade pressed against Tall Cancer Beard's neck, Blood demanded he drop his rifle.

He did it. No questions posed.

Short Beer Gut turned, aimed his rifle for Blood.

I triggered a round from the AR-15 at his booted feet. He screamed and his dog ran off. Man's best friend. 'Til the going got tough.

"Don't shoot! Don't shoot!" he yelped, dropping his rifle.

Eyes shifting to Tall Cancer Beard, I could see a wet stain forming on his midsection. The stain grew bigger and bigger with each passing second.

"Now," Blood said. "Both you two hillbilly racists strip down."

They glanced at one another.

"Whaddya mean strip down?" Short Beer Gut said.

"You know what it means," Blood said.

I gathered up both their rifles, ejected the ammo, and slammed the stocks against the nearest tree-trunk, shattering them. They both looked like they were about to burst into tears.

"Hunt's over for you two," I said. "Now do like my brother says and strip down."

"Start with your boots," Blood added.

The two of them reluctantly bent over, untied their boots, kicked them off.

"Now the pants," Blood insisted.

"You ain't planning on doing anything to us when we naked, are you?" inquired Tall Cancer Beard.

"You mean like something that goes down inside Dannemora?" Blood said.

"You'll just have to wait and see now, won't you?" I said, shooting my partner a wink. Then, "Whaddaya think, Blood? The pudgy one's got a *perty* mouth."

I could see real fear in Short Beer Gut's face. He started to cry.

"Strip down," Blood insisted. "Now."

He then shifted the knife and ran it down the back of Tall Cancer Beard's camo patterned jacket. The jacket slid off the bean pole in two separate halves. The move lit a fire under them, and they stripped down. That was when Blood pressed the AR-15 stock against his shoulder, shifting his aim slowly from one man to the other.

"Now go," he said.

They both exchanged glances.

"Go where?" said Short Beer Gut. "We ain't got no clothes."

Blood fired a round that took even me by surprise. He wasn't fucking around. Not with two grown men who thought nothing of referring to a black man as a spook.

Tears running down Short Beer Gut's face, he sprinted across the clearing and into the thick woods. When Tall Cancer Beard realized he was the last one standing, he too, turned and ran into the woods.

That left me alone with Blood. His eyes locked onto my own. He fell silent for a long beat, until he worked up a sly smile. I smiled too, but quickly the smile turned into laughter. The good times, however, weren't to be had for long. Blood raised his right hand, and with extended index finger, pointed at the metal access door.

"They down in there," he said under his breath. "Them two cons. I can feel it."

"Me too," I said. "Question is, how do we get the rats out of the rat hole?"

CHAPTER 26

I met Blood on the opposite side of the clearing.

"Way I see it," I said, "we've got two choices."

"I'd say I'm all ears, if there wasn't so much more of me to offer."

"We either try that door, see if it's open."

"And if it's open?"

"We go in guns ablazin'."

"Guns ablazin'. Did you just say that?"

I nodded. "Or, we think this one through a little more, for safety's sake."

"I like option number two," Blood said.

We paused to think about it for a minute. Then, without saying another word, I made my way back to the metal door, wrapped my hand around the lever.

"Careful," Blood said. "Could be booby trapped."

The two cons were smart enough to pull off a daring if not

complicated escape out of one of the most secure prisons in the country. It wouldn't be all that far-fetched to imagine their having planted some kind of explosive device that would detonate as soon as I pulled on the lever. But time was tight. If those two local yokels were any indication, D'Amico and his men would be closing in on this position soon. Sooner than soon. Add to that Agent Muscolino's promise that the FBI would be taking over later this afternoon, and I was about to lose total control of the situation. I promised to deliver two escaped cons for Governor Valente and that was what I planned on doing. Keeper the trustworthy.

I pulled up on the lever. It moved slightly. But something was obstructing it from performing its intended function. Something metal and strong by the sound of it.

I stood up.

"It's padlocked from the inside," I said.

"And if it's padlocked from the inside," Blood said, like a question.

"Then without question, Moss and Sweet are home sweet home."

We stood there for another long moment. Mother Nature surrounded us. Song birds singing, cicadas buzzing in the trees, spiders making webs, snakes in the grass, the breeze blowing through the leaves. It was like living inside Hallmark card. But down inside that hole were a couple of rats. And we needed to figure out a way to smoke them out.

Smoke them out...

"I think I have an idea," I said.

"'Bout time," Blood said. "I was getting bored."

"If they're underground, it only makes sense they'd require some kind of air circulation system."

He pressed his lips together. The gesture meant he could already see where I was going with this.

"Still carry your zippo, non-smoker?" he said.

I pulled it out of my cargo pants pocket, flicked open the lid.

"Now we just gotta find the vent. Or vents."

We split up, Blood taking one side of the clearing and me taking the other. We didn't find any air vents in the clearing, but once we started searching the tall grass, we came upon two separate, T-shaped aluminum vents that stuck six inches out of the ground. The openings were horizontal to the ground to prevent rainwater from getting into them, and they were covered with protective screens to keep out the critters, both big and small.

"You got your Gerber, Blood?"

He retrieved the multi-tool instrument from the holster attached to his belt, handed it to me. I accessed the screwdriver and began removing the four screws from the first screen. Then, working as quietly as possible, removed the second screen.

"We need something flammable."

"Leave that to me," Blood said. He gathered up a small pile of dead leaves and branches that didn't catch much of a soaking during the day's earlier thunderstorm. He then filled the two hillbilly hunter camo-patterned shirts with the flammable material.

"How much lighter fluid you got in that Zippo?" he said.

I peered down at the silver-plated lighter. It had been a birthday gift from my wife, Fran, back when we were first married. It had my initials embossed into the metal. JHM. Jack Harrison Marconi. The three letters had faded a bit over the many years since I'd first laid eyes on the lighter. Wear and tear will do that to a soft metal. But the memory of Fran hadn't faded one bit. Her long dark hair, brown eyes, and funny smile still dominated my mind with full clarity. I could even still smell her lavender scent. That kind of true love never died, even if the body has been reclaimed by heaven and earth.

"You okay, Keep?"

I shook my head.

"Yeah," I said, feeling the weight of the lighter in the palm of my hand and the heavy weight of Fran's memory in my mind and in my heart. I didn't smoke anymore, which meant the device contained plenty of fluid. I pulled a coin from my pocket, unscrewed the small bottom access piece until it was loose enough for me to remove it with my fingertips. Then, placing my thumb loosely over the little round hole, I sprinkled some of the fluid onto both shirts, like holy water on a priest's cassock. When I was done, I still had at least a third of the fluid left inside the lighter. I screwed the fuel access piece back onto the bottom, then flicked open the lighter lid, pressed my thumb against the black flint.

"Ready?" I said, holding the lighter up like I was about to pull the pin on a grenade.

Blood nodded.

I thumbed the flint and produced a tall flame. I touched the shirts with the flame.

CHAPTER 27

Their necks are starting to hurt from staring up at the metal door.

"You think they're gone?" Sweet says, the blood from his throbbing thumb wound running down his forearm so that every minute or so he's forced to wipe it away with a filthy dish rag. "You know what we need, Picasso? We need ourselves one of those periscopes like they use on the nuclear submarines that run under the ice at the North Pole. Then we could periscope up and see exactly who we're dealing with. Make a surprise attack."

The pain in Moss's leg is beginning to ease. Rather, he's bleeding so badly now, that a pool of his dark red DNA has formed on the floor directly beneath his chair. The blood-letting is making him feel woozy and drugged. The pain that had been stabbing at his nervous system with every beat of his heart just moments ago is now replaced with a feeling of almost euphoria.

"Question is, asshole," he says, "how do you get that periscope up *through a layer of ice that must be a hundred feet thick?"*

Sweet bleeds, stares at his partner like he just farted something wet and foul.

"Can you for fucking once just go with something I say? Can you just for once accept it for what it is and not analyze the fucking living snot out of it? Can you just give me a little fucking credit for once?"

Moss smiles.

"I'll give credit when the credit is due, asshole. And right now, the only credit I can give you is for being an asshole...a stupid, dumb fuck, computer geek asshole."

The throbbing in Sweet's right hand is so bad, it feels like a blood-filled balloon that's about to pop all over his chest and face. How the fuck is it going to be possible for him to hold a rifle or a shotgun? At least he's got his left hand to work with. He uses the hand to reach for the riot shotgun laid out on the tabletop, grabbing it by the pump, cocking the weapon one-handed by snapping it up and down, John Wayne style. He then turns the barrel on Moss while he shifts his hand from the pump lever to the trigger grip.

"Apologize," he says.

Moss looks at him for an extended beat. Then, feeling himself growing a smile, he starts to laugh.

"Now that's funny, stupid periscope-up-against-the-ice asshole."

Sweet stands fast, kicking the chair out from under him. "Apologize."

"What, you say something, asshole?"

"Apologize, Picasso. Or I'm going to blow your brains out."

Moss laughs some more. "You and me, asshole. In case you hadn't already noticed. We're fucking as good as dead. No Mexico, no sandy beach, no crystal clear blue water, no seniorita tettas in your mouth, no freedom, no Shawshank Redemption of any kind whatso-fucking-ever. So what difference is it going to make at this point if you blow me back to hell?"

A single, sad tear falls down Sweet's cheek. Heart pounding in his throat, he feels the weight of the shotgun in his awkward hand, feels his finger on the trigger, and he's amazed to see the lack of fear in his partner's face. It's almost like the son of a bitch wants to die.

Sweet sniffles, swallows a wad of bitter-tasting post-nasal drip.

"Well, well, Picasso," he says, "if you wanna die that bad."

Extending his shooting arm, he aims the barrel at Moss's stubbly, round face. Pointblank. But Moss is laughing so hard now, he can't get a breath. He's going to pass out.

"Shut up!" Sweet shouts. "Shut up! Shut! Up! Shut the fuck up!"

The cloud of smoke becomes noticeable then. It's beginning to pour into the room from two different places. From the vent opening directly to Sweet's right-hand side and from the identical ceiling-mounted vent on his left-hand side.

"What the fuck is that?" he says.

Moss's smile fades. He suddenly finds himself perked up, and along with it, the severe pain returning to his shattered leg.

"They're trying to smoke us out."

The smoke pours in, and along with it, the oxygen replaced with toxic air.

Sweet starts coughing. "Jesus, I can't fucking breathe."

He jogs over to the vent on his right, aims the barrel of the shotgun at the vent, fires. The round of heavy buckshot blows a hole into the acoustic ceiling, and at the same time, causes the source of the smoke to catch fire. The fire immediately spreads to the old, dried out ceiling tiles.

"Nice going, asshole," Moss says. "Now we're on fire. Maybe we should periscope up, see if the coast is clear."

"Shut up, Picasso!" he screams. "For once, shut the fuck up!"

The smoke spreads so thick it's blinding. If not for the fire, the place would be entirely fogged in with a thick gray-black toxic cloud.

"We gotta get out of here," Sweet says. "We gotta leave."

"I can't make it," Moss says. "You go. Shoot whoever is doing this, and leave the hatch open. I'll get out on my own. Go, get lost. Be gone, asshole."

Sweet looks at his partner. It's hard to see his face through the smoke. But he sees it well enough.

"You don't have to tell me twice, Picasso," he says, dropping the shotgun back onto the table and shoving one of the pistol barrels into his belt. Digging for the padlock key in his pocket, he makes his way to the steel ladder. "Been nice knowing you, fat cock. Have a nice life, and an even nicer slow death." He laughs, then sings, "I'm going to Mex-i-coooo," to the tune of the 90s' Dada classic, I'm Going to Dizz Knee Land…

Climbing the ladder, Sweet unlocks the padlock. Pushing the steel hatch open, he looks one way and then the other. But the last thing Moss sees before passing out from smoke inhalation is Sweet's gun falling through the thick gray cloud, slow motion, to the shelter floor.

CHAPTER 28

Blood was waiting for Sweet as soon as he stuck his head out of the opening and stole a deep cleansing breath, free from the black gray smoke that was also rising up out of the opening, like the exhaust on a coal-fired locomotive smokestack. It was like playing whack-a-mole at the local arcade. Only in this case, whack-a-fucking-rat. Using the butt of his AR-15 like a battering ram, he smacked the pistol out of the escaped con's hand. The pistol dropped down into the shaft. Then, grabbing the rat's shirt collar with his free hand, Blood yanked him out of the hole, tossing him to the clearing floor.

"Jesus Christ!" Sweet barked. "You're a freakin' monster."

Blood pointed the barrel on the AR-15 at him. "Stay down. We not through here."

From down on his back, Sweet raised his hands in surrender. Rather, he raised his left hand and what was left of his right hand.

"Easy, man," he said. Then, trying to work up a smile, "Or should I say, easy *brother*. You and me, man, we like brothers. You know, black and brown against the town."

Blood triggered a round off over his head. "Nothin' brown or black about you, jerk."

"Okay! Okay!" Sweet shouted. "Go easy, man. I'm injured. I need a hospital, like real bad."

"Shut your mouth," Blood said.

I pulled back the slide on the AR-15, held it securely by its hard rubber pistol grip, and stepped down into the opening.

"Sure you don't want me to go down the rat hole?" Blood said. "You need an oxygen mask."

"Thanks for the offer, but I need you to watch Sweet. All goes well, we're out of here in a minute. Two at most. Dinner with the girls, remember?"

Blood nodded, cracked a hint of grin. "Watch your back."

"If I could, I would," I said. Then I descended into the hole.

The smoke had thinned now that the rooftop hatch was opened. But the place was ablaze. When I came to the bottom, I could see that most of the ceiling had caught fire.

"Reginald Moss!" I shouted. "I know you're down here. There's no point in trying to hide. You can either stay here and burn, or you can come with me. I promise, you'll be safe."

The pistol barrel poked the back of my skull.

"Down on your knees," he said, following with a cough that sounded like his lungs were about to bleed out his nostrils. He was still groggy from having passed out for a minute or two. "And drop the rifle."

The fire was spreading, the burning tile embers raining down on our heads. In a few seconds the wood wall finishes, rugs, and furniture would catch and we'd be lucky to make it out alive before the whole thing flashed. I dropped the weapon, put my hands on my head, locking them at the knuckles, and slowly lowered myself to my knees. He shifted the pistol barrel so that now it painfully prodded my cranial cap.

"What do you want, Moss?" I said. "You haven't got a chance if you kill me. No way you're climbing out of that shaft alone. You're only option is to trust me. Let me take you in. I'll see to it you're treated fairly."

"Who are you?" he shouted. "You FBI?"

"Not at all," I barked, the smoke and heat from the flames burning the back of my throat. "I'm a private detective."

He laughed. "A private investigator. Who the fuck sent you?" Then, as if already knowing the answer to his own question, "He sent you, didn't he? The governor? He sent you personally. Bet he wants me alive just so he can make sure without a doubt that I'm dead. Dead and so very fucking silent."

I had to admit, it was a good guess. But why would his thought process immediately link me to Governor Valente? Reginald Moss would already have to have something connecting him to the governor for that to happen. But what could those two possibly have in common? A major political figure and a convicted murderer? And why would Valente want Moss dead?

I lowered my head, and stared at the floor. The lower I got, the easier it was to breathe. I noticed something out the corner of my eye then. Richard's leg. It was bleeding badly. In fact, the leg was severely busted up, like some heavy machinery had run it over. It looked like a broken tree branch. He wasn't standing directly on it. He supported the bulk of his weight instead with the use of a crutch.

I didn't hesitate. Cocking my elbow, I buried it in the damaged leg.

The sound that emerged from his mouth was more than just a scream. It was like an eruption. A primal scream that originated not from his lungs, but from deep down inside a soul blackened by fire and smoke, and also by an evil so profound it belonged only to hell. He discharged the pistol as he fell back, the round ricocheting off the wall. I flipped over onto my stomach, grabbed the AR-15 and fired three back-to-back rounds. One of the rounds ricocheted off two walls, and another connected with his shoulder, blowing a chunk of flesh and bone out of it. But that didn't stop him from firing at me again, the bullets whizzing over my head like wasps. I triggered two more rounds that nailed the wall behind him. He fired again, the round grazing my shoulder.

The fire spread down along the walls then, the heat inside the small room intense and unbearable. Like an oven on broil. He fired again, this time shuffling himself towards me, his face bearing a broad smile, like he was having fun while dying.

I planted a bead on him, pressed the trigger. But it jammed. I tried slamming the housing with the ball of my hand, but it was no use. I tossed the weapon at him, but it fell short and slid across the concrete floor.

He shuffled himself closer to me, his smile having grown even wider.

"Good news," he barked. "Looks like we're going to hell in a handbasket together." He cocked the hammer back with his thumb, wrapped his finger around the trigger.

"Speak for yourself, you son of a bitch," I said, pulling the .45 from my shoulder holster, and shooting him between the eyes.

I crawled my way to Moss's body. Pulled what I could from his pockets, including a wallet and what could only be a counterfeit passport. Shoving them into my cargo pants pocket, I went to the ladder, just as the fire began to consume all the walls. It was a mistake to grab hold of the rungs with my bare hands, because the hot metal nearly melted the skin.

Making my way quickly back to Moss, I ripped the shirt off his back. I covered my hands with it, then shuffled back to the ladder. I could still feel the heat coming from the fire-baked rungs while I climbed. I was three or four rungs from the top when the fire flashed, and I was blown out of the hole, like a human cannon ball out of a cannon.

I lay on my back on the damp ground, looking up at Blood. He stood over me, looking big and strong, like a dark Adirondack Mountain, a smile plastered on his face.

"Where's the AR-15?" he said. "Don't tell me you left it down there. That was a loan."

"I'm fine, Blood," I said. "Thanks for your concern."

I stood up, assessed the damage. Nothing on fire as far as I could see. Nothing too terribly burnt. Not even the palms of my hands, although they would no doubt blister up. My shoulder felt like hell though, and when I touched it, blood came away on my fingers. Reaching into my pocket I pulled out my kerchief, shoved it into the open neck on my T-shirt, shifted it to my right arm, pressed it against the slight grazing. The wound stung, but I'd live.

Down on his knees a few feet away from me, was Derrick Sweet, the lone survivor of the two escaped convicts. His right hand looked like it'd been shoved through a meat grinder and his thin, if not gaunt, scruffy face looked pale and defeated.

"Who are you guys?" he said.

"We're your new best friends," I said.

Then I told him our names and that we weren't the law. That we were freelancers working for a private contractor.

"Our job was to capture you both alive, and do so before the state troopers or the FBI do."

"Looks like you fucked up by half," he said.

Blood looked at me. "The con can count."

I thought about what he said. About Moss dying down there in that hell hole. And I suddenly felt a wave of guilt pass through me. His death, although warranted, was on me and me alone. I'd failed. Valente would be none too happy about that. In a way justice had been served. But that was only in terms of the law. Both New York State's version of it and God's. In terms of the job I agreed to take on for the governor however, I was one short of a perfect pair. I wondered if it meant I was slipping, or simply getting old, or that in this case anyway, circumstances beyond my control prevented me from capturing Moss alive. Maybe in the end, it meant only one thing: Valente would now be missing out on a PR opportunity for parading both escaped convicts on live TV.

"So who hired you?" Sweet said.

"None of your business," Blood said. Then, grabbing hold of the convict's collar, he pulled him up off the ground. "Let's get moving," he added. "Before more of the local yokels come out of the woodwork, attempt to steal you for the one hundred grand."

"Fifty grand," I said. "Do the math."

CHAPTER 29

We started walking back in the direction of home. It was slow going through the thick stuff. By the time we made it out onto the railroad bed, we were coated in a layer of sweat. Sweet was breathing heavily and tightly gripping the wrist on his mutilated hand. He was still bleeding and, for a moment, I thought he, too, might not make it. Which would make our mission a complete bust.

"You never told me who you work for," he said as we walked in the middle of the bed, single file. Me out front, the con in the middle, Blood taking up the rear, his AR-15 at the ready should the bad guy decide to make a run for it through the woods.

"Does it matter?" I said.

"It's the governor, ain't it?"

I felt a start in my heart. Moss had guessed the same thing without my dropping any hints whatsoever as to who might be paying me for my services. When I didn't answer, I heard him snicker.

"Yup," he said, "it's Valente. You see, Mister, ummm, what did you say your names were again?"

"We didn't," Blood said.

"That's okay, Blood," I said. "Maybe we should mind our manners after all." Speaking over my shoulder, I said, "I'm Keeper Marconi, and this is my associate, Blood. Blood is bad ass. He also bites the heads off rats. So be careful."

Blood rolled his eyes, snickered.

"I've already decided not to mess with Mr. Blood," Sweet said. "Where'd you get a name like Keeper?"

"The real name is Jack. But way back when, when I was the warden at Green Haven Max, the inmates started calling me Keeper and it stuck."

"A former warden. Now this is really beginning to make sense."

Another start in my heart. Something was up. What precisely was up, I couldn't yet put my finger on it. But it most definitely had to do with my employer and, if my gut served me right, some crucial information he was hiding from me.

"What he talking about, Keep?" Blood said.

"Not sure yet, Blood. But I'm sure Mr. Sweet won't mind opening up about it on the drive back home."

"Where's home?" Sweet said.

"Dannemora Prison," I said. "Solitary confinement. By way of Clinton County lockup."

Back at the 4Runner, we sat Sweet in the back seat. Blood took the seat beside him, both his big hands still gripping his semi-automatic rifle. I got behind the wheel and pulled out of the secluded spot. Pulling out my cell phone, I called Bridgette, told her we were coming in, and to be ready for us. She asked me if I had both men. I told her we only had one. She sighed, asked me what happened. "Unfortunate accident," I said. I felt the pain in my shoulder and I could practically smell the blood leaking from Sweet's finger and told her we'd need some emergency medical assistance.

"No press," I said. "I don't want anyone knowing we're bringing Sweet in."

"When you get to the sheriff's office," she said, "pull up around back. No one will see you there. Or suspect anything."

I hung up, concentrated on the rural road.

"Why do you keep asking me if the governor is my employer, Sweet?" I said.

"Why you wanna know?" he said, his tone caked with sarcasm. "You're not the cops, Keeper. It's none of your business."

This was where things got a little fuzzy for me. Sweet was right. He might be an asshole, but his relationship with the governor…his and Moss's…truly fell within the category of none-of-my-damned-business. I'd been hired to find Sweet and Moss and then deliver them, alive, to Valente's Albany, Eagle Street address. I hadn't been hired to look into my employer's relationship with the escapees and what the relationship might entail, even if it turned out to be illegal.

Problem was, I couldn't help myself when it came to right and wrong. In other words, if the governor was engaged in some kind of illegal activity with the two cons, as crazy as it sounded, then maybe

I had a moral obligation to get to the bottom of it. For better or for worse.

"How do you know it's none of my business?" I said.

"I'm guessing Valente hired you because you and the monster back there, who I'm guessing is an ex-con because I can smell one from a mile away, know prisons and screws and inmates. You also know all about our habits."

"For instance?"

"For instance, Keeper," he said, "you knew we wouldn't be in Mexico yet. That we'd lay low for a while until the state troopers gave up their fuck-all-ridiculous search, and the FBI came in and expanded it to other states."

"That would be the time to move," I said. "When the eyes weren't focused on you anymore."

"That was the plan."

"But your plan didn't work," said, Blood. "Joyce ditched your ass. Mean Gene ratted you out. And now you're on your way back to the pen via the governor. To rot."

"Maybe," Sweet said.

"Maybe," I said. "Maybe is not an option."

"Maybe I don't go back to the pen," he said. "Maybe instead, we make a little deal."

"You make a deal with us," I said. "Now that's rich, buddy."

He exhaled. "What would you say if I offered you three hundred thousand cash to split between the two of you?"

I locked eyes with Blood in the rearview. He winked.

"We listening," my partner said.

Sweet was holding his wrist. His damaged hand was so swollen, it looked like it was going to explode in a haze of blood, puss, and rotted flesh.

"Money talks," he said.

Then he told us his plan.

CHAPTER 30

So here's what we found out about the madness going down inside the depths of Dannemora Prison. Turned out the voices we heard inside the prison, the high-pitched wails, weren't just figments of our imagination, or breeding cats for that matter. Because if what Sweet revealed to me and Blood bore even a semblance of truth, Dannemora wasn't just a place for incarcerating a few thousand dangerous convicts, it was also a place that made some serious casheshe on the black market. In fact, the place was a goddamned money factory.

Once more I looked Blood in the eye. His eyes were wide, unblinking and intense, as if to say, *"Can you believe the shit this guy is telling us?"*

Here's the short of it: according to Sweet, the basement, dungeon depths of Dannemora, or what affectionately had been dubbed the Crypt, was being utilized not only as a meth lab, but also as a ground zero for child sex trafficking.

Sweet said, "The kids are pulled off the street. Runaways most of them. Or they hire a teenage kid to act as a front man. A kid maybe sixteen or seventeen. He pretends to be a thirteen-year-old girl's boyfriend, maybe take her out to dinner and then go for a drive in the country. That drive might end up in a section of woods outside Dannemora, and that's where the fuckers pounce on them. Once inside the prison, they keep them locked away where no one knows about them other than a select group of trusted people. Some of the big time meth buyers are offered first dibs."

Sweet had no way of being aware of it, but I'd managed to pull out my phone while turning on the recording application. I couldn't be sure I was getting everything that spilled from his mouth, but it was worth a shot.

"Who's they?" Blood asked. "The *fuckers* you speak of."

"Rodney Pappas. His select band of merry on-the-take screws. His little secret Crypt army."

"Go figure," I said.

"You'd be surprised how much a thirteen-year-old boy or girl goes for on the black market. What a sixty-year-old man might drop for one of those kids besides his BVDs. Then, when they're through, the kids are shipped across the country to another site. It's an entire network of trafficking and a lot of it is occurring inside maximum security prisons. They all talk to one another."

"Just how lucrative is this business?" I asked, my stomach twisting and sickened by his confession, however true or false. That said, his description was too detailed for him to be lying. So the question that loomed large was this: how could the warden of Dannemora Prison not be aware of the evil that lurked inside the depths of his own iron house?

The answer hit me upside the head. Clark did know about the human trafficking and drug lab because he was facilitating it. It was the only explanation that made any sense.

"Profits for Dannemora alone are in the tens of millions," Sweet said. "But that's just a guesstimate."

"So you're in on it?" I said.

"More than a few inmates are in on it. I was a small time player in the racket. So was Moss. We were like soldiers or slaves, depending on your point of view. Paid to do what we were told to do. It beat the shit out of sitting inside our cells all day."

"Paid how?" Blood interjected.

"Meth mostly," he said. "Sometimes cash. There was the offer of sex with one of those kids, but you gotta be one sick fuck to get into that kind of thing."

"Joyce and Mean Gene? They in on it too?" Blood said.

"Excellent, Blood man," he said, "you pick up fast."

"So what'd you have in mind?" I pushed. "What's your plan?"

"More like an offer," he said. "You don't put me back in that prison, I'll make sure you guys collect. Collect big time. Three hundred K."

"I'm not putting you back in prison," I said. "First we head to the jail to get patched up, then I'm delivering you to the governor as planned."

"Either way," Sweet said, "I'm a dead man. Don't you get it?"

"Get what?" I said, eyes back in the rearview, eyeing both Blood and the con.

"The fucking governor," he said, laughing despite the pain in his hand. "The Dannemora Crypt is his personal pet project."

Up ahead, the gray concrete walls of the Clinton County Sheriff's Department loomed large. I told Sweet to get down, become invisible. Then I pulled into the lot past the sea of reporters and gawkers and drove around back. The back was fenced in, but the electronic lock had been triggered from the inside and the gate was already open in anticipation of our arrival. After we pulled in, the gate automatically closed back up. I drove up to the back solid metal door. It opened, and Karla came rushing out.

"Saw you coming," she said as I stepped out of the Toyota. "The medics are on their way. Are you hurt bad?"

"Not me, but our guest is on his way out, we don't get him patched up."

The rear driver's side door on the 4Runner opened, and Blood quickly dragged Sweet out by the collar before anyone noticed. The con looked like forty miles of chewed up roadway. Karla opened the facility's back metal door and we entered the jailhouse just as the reporters flocked to the back gates like hungry vultures.

I found Bridgette standing outside the four jail cells.

"You okay?" she said. There was a look of genuine concern on her face. "The paramedics are almost here."

"I know," I said. "Karla told me."

Sweet was placed inside cell number three, the door locked behind him. That was when I turned to Bridgette.

"We need to talk," I said. "You, me, and Blood. In your office."

"By all means," she said. "I'll make some coffee."

"Whiskey would be better," Blood said.

CHAPTER 31

I t didn't come as a surprise that Bridgette Hylton enjoyed a nip or two during the day. Which was why she kept a bottle of Jack Daniels in her bottom desk drawer. Rather, an "emergency bottle," as she referred to it. We stood around her desk drinking the whiskey from yellow Dixie cups, while I recapped not only the capture of the Moss and Sweet down in that backwoods bomb shelter, but also what Sweet relayed to me about the child trafficking and drug running going on in the depths of Dannemora Prison. Inside a place Sweet ominously called the Crypt. I also played her the recording of Sweet's statement with the smartphone recording app.

She poured us another shot of whiskey apiece.

"Those reporters out there have no idea you just brought Sweet in," she said. "Or else they'd be tossing rocks through the windows trying to get in. They also don't know that Moss is dead. I need to alert D'Amico on both counts just for starters. You know that, right?"

I nodded.

"FBI needs to know also," I said. "But here's the catch. I tell my employer the news, he's liable to take control of the situation."

"What's that mean?" Bridgette said.

"What I mean is, what if Valente is involved in the drug-slash-human trafficking ring? In fact, what if he's the major player?"

"He gonna wanna protect his assets," Blood interjected while pouring himself a third shot. "Some politicians become governors as a stepping stone to the Presidency of the United States of America. Maybe Valente choose to be governor so he can make himself tens of millions of non-taxable dollars."

"Stranger stories have been told, Blood."

The sheriff looked at me with a tight face. A face that was feeling the effects of stress over two escaped convicts. But ironically, now that one of them was dead and the other recaptured, she seemed even more stressed.

"So what is it you want to do?" she asked.

"Here's what I'm thinking," I said. "Maude's dead, which means we already have one murder we can link directly to the illicit activity going on in the prison."

"In other words," Blood said, "some key players in this thing never intended for us to find Moss and Sweet in the first place. Key players who are supposed to be on our team. The A team."

Bridgette drank down what remained of the whiskey in her cup. She crushed the cup in her hand, tossed it into the metal waste paper basket.

"I don't report Moss dead and Sweet captured, I lose my job," she said. "As it is, I need to get a forensics team out to the site of his death."

"But we can use Sweet to expose what's happening inside the Crypt. You do that, you not only keep your job, you get a nice shiny new star."

She smiled. "Oh, well, I guess I never thought of that. A nice new star. You got a plan for exposing the so-called drug-slash-human trafficking ring inside the prison dungeon?"

"Crypt," Blood corrected her.

"Crypt," she repeated.

"I do," I said. I drank the rest of my whiskey, crushed the cup in the palm of my hand. "But it's going to involve making a deal with Sweet. Probably his freedom or something close, for his cooperation."

She shook her head. "How are we going to manage that if we keep his capture a secret? We'd have to make an official appeal to the DA and the courts."

"Obviously that would take hours. So what you do instead is have the lovely Karla write up an offer that Sweet can live with. Then the two of you sign it."

"What then?" Blood said.

"Then we come to the good part. You familiar with the Biblical story of the Prodigal Son, Bridgette?"

"The wayward son unexpectedly returns home."

"Derrick Sweet is going to be our personal Prodigal Son," I said, tossing my crushed cup into the basket.

CHAPTER 32

He sits on the edge of the stainless steel cot inside his small cell and feels the electrical pulse-like throbs of pain shoot up and down his arm. The thumb has turned black under the two blood-encrusted and useless butterfly bandages. Every now and then, a little spurt of blood shoots through the moist, thick, scaly purple and black scab. But the pain is nothing compared to his disappointment. No, scratch that. Not his disappointment. Rather, his fury. Fury at himself for following Picasso around like a little dog with a ring through his nose instead of doing the right thing, the smart thing, and taking off for Mexico as soon as they busted out of that shit-filled sewer pipe. So what if Joyce never showed up to provide them the help they'd need for getting south of the border? It was just as well she didn't show up. It meant they didn't have to waste time killing her retarded husband. It meant they could separate and may the best man make it to the border first.

But he didn't go with his gut. Instead he listened to Moss. Listened to him when he insisted they lay low at the established underground safe house. Lay low until the state troopers gave up on the local search, abandoned the road blocks and the cabin-by-cabin searches for something much broader, something much more porous. Only then did they stand the chance of slipping through the cracks, and even then, only if they were very lucky would they stand a reasonably decent chance of making it to Mexico. But they had to stick together, work together, back one another up. Be a team. Be as one.

Bullshit.

See what happens when your stick together? You end up stepping in a goddamned bear trap. You end up getting your fucking thumb chopped off. You end up getting smoked out of your hole, and you end up getting burned alive. Then, and only then, after you've suffered the physical torture, do you get your ass caught by a couple of private investigators who think they're the fucking Lone Ranger and his trusty sidekick, Black Tonto.

But if there's a bright side in this shit storm, it's this: men and women can be bought. Especially private detectives. Half of them are drunk or on their way to getting there anyway. All it will take to get them to agree on a plan that will ultimately lead to his grand prize of a permanent Mexican beach vacation, is three hundred thousand dollars. That's gotta be way more than Valente was gonna pay them off. But here's the catch: in order to get the money, he's gotta get back inside the joint, get himself back down into the Crypt, head directly to the vault. He's gotta pull off a break-in. And soon as he gets his hands on the cash, he's got to once more break out. It's the only possible way out of this mess and it's the only alternative. Because if he goes back to Valente directly, he's a dead man. If he is released back into Dannemora officially as a captured fugitive, he's *a dead man. At the same time, if he tries to escape the Clinton County Jail, they'll shoot him on sight. No matter how you shake it up, he's dead and buried.*

The only choice is to cut a private deal, pay for it with cash from the Crypt, hope for the best.

Then, the sound of the back door opening. Boot steps. Jackboot steps, combined with the sound of voices. Manly voices.

"You take four, I got one and two. No survivors…"

Eyes wide, he thrusts himself up against the interior wall so that he can't be seen if one of these jackbooted assholes peeks in through the narrow door glass. He makes out the unmistakable sound of automatic weapons being locked and loaded. Gun metal against gun metal. Followed by the shock and awe of dozens of rounds being fired through sound suppressed barrels. He hears glass shattering. Safety glass. He makes out screams. Female and male screams. The violent attack rocks his brain, nearly causes his ticker to stop pumping blood and oxygen.

What the fuck is happening?

They're using high-powered semi-automatic weapons equipped with sound suppressors, like they don't want the press to have a clue about the murders. It's like the military or Clinton County SWAT has taken the law into their own hands. But he knows full well what the fuck is happening. Because no way would the military or SWAT be shooting the joint up.

It's Rodney and his men.

"The motherfuckers have come to kill us all," he whispers to himself. "Silence us. But Rodney doesn't know I'm here. Or does he?"

The cell door bursts open, a rifle butt raised high…

CHAPTER 33

oise coming from the cell bay. Breaking glass. Screaming. Shouting.
A series of short, sharp pops that I immediately translated as
suppressed semi-automatic gunfire. The kind of noise that pierces
the flesh as much as the metal jacketed rounds. Pulling my .45 from the
shoulder holster, I ran out into the general office area only to see Karla
standing in the middle of the floor, her face pale with panic.

"I thought it was the paramedics. They drove up in an EMT truck.
Like the real thing. I let them in through the back gate."

"If you got a sidearm," I said, "now's the time to use it."

Blood ran out of the office, on my heels. Bridgette was directly
behind him. They both had guns gripped in their hands, combat
position. Pressing my back up against the wall before making my way
into the corridor that accessed the cells, I raised my left hand up for
Blood to clearly see. I extended three fingers. Dropping the first, he
assumed a position directly beside me. I dropped a second finger.

"I aim high," he whispered, his voice steady, breathing even, not labored. "You go low."

The third finger dropped.

We entered into the corridor just as two figures dressed in black, including black ski masks, began making their way for the back door. They'd taken a man hostage. Sweet. They both turned long enough to squeeze out a couple of wild rounds at us. Blood and I stood our ground, returned the fire while trying to avoid nailing Sweet in the cross-fire. I nailed the second man in the leg. He screamed and released his grip on Sweet. The con dropped to the concrete floor like a sad bag of bones. The two intruders didn't dare attempt to retrieve their prize. The uninjured man grabbed hold of his injured partner, made for the back door. Blood and I fired again, but it was too late. They were already through the door.

We gave chase. But the back solid metal door wouldn't budge. Something was jammed in the exterior opener. Maybe a piece of two by four pressed up against the underside of the exterior latch. Or maybe a steel chair-back shoved up against it.

"Son of a bitch!" Me shouting.

Bridgette and Karla were positioned behind us now.

"Karla!" I shouted. "Close the gate. Now!"

She ran out and back into the general area. But through the door I could make out the truck engine revving, RPMs peaking, truck motor firing up, tires spitting gravel. And I knew our efforts to capture the bastards was futile and stupid.

"Stand down everyone," I said, returning the .45 to its holster. "Check on the prisoners."

"Ain't gonna be much left to check on," Blood said.

"Call D'Amico," I said to Bridgette, "and tell him Clinton County Lockup is under siege."

CHAPTER 34

O f course they were dead. Three of them, that is. Black Widow Joyce, her loyal-to-the-death husband, Larry, and Mean Gene Bender. Miraculously, Derrick Sweet managed to survive. Although the extent of his thumb wound was getting so bad, it would be a miracle if he didn't lose his hand.

I turned to Sheriff Hylton. "This has turned into a hell of a lot more than just a couple of escaped cons. This is about some serious bad shit going on in Dannemora max. Those invading bastards might have been wearing ski masks, but you and I both know that the big one was Rodney. We've got to scale the fortress walls, expose the Crypt to the world, before more kids get violated, or die."

"D'Amico is on his way," she said. "It's his call."

"This your town," Blood said. "You make the call."

"The more we stall," I said, "the better chance Rodney, Clark, and Valente have of whitewashing the Crypt operation. We need to get there now, while it's in working order."

Outside the facility, the sound of emergency sirens. Fire, EMTs. The back door burst open once more. Men dressed in ballistic gear marched in. They were the good guys this time.

"Down on the floor!" the lead man shouted.

You didn't fuck with these guys.

Blood and I dropped our weapons, went down onto floor.

"Hands over your head!"

We did as they told us.

"I'm the sheriff," Bridgette said, while she too dropped down, setting her side-arm onto the concrete floor. "You know exactly who I am."

A man squeezed through the crowd. A short man with a solid build and an angry as all hell face.

D'Amico.

CHAPTER 35

While EMTs and Clinton County Forensics worked the scene of the killings, Blood, Bridgette, and myself occupied her office. D'Amico stood foursquare on the floor. Blood and I sat on the couch, sipping more of Bridgette's whiskey. She, too, sipped a whiskey while sitting back in her swivel chair.

"That's against regulations," D'Amico said.

"You ain't the boss of me," I said.

Blood stood up tall. Taller than tall. He stood not beside D'Amico, but up against him. The trooper came up to the center of Blood's sternum. He looked uncomfortable. Intimidated. I thought he might pee himself.

"Let me guess," Blood said. "This be the part where you tell us we had no business going after them two escaped cons on our own."

D'Amico stood his ground, looked directly up at Blood's face. David and Goliath.

"You willfully interfered with a state police investigation," he said. "And now one of the two is dead and the other's nearly dead. The two... no, make that three corroborating witnesses are dead, and now Clinton County is under siege by some rogue gang who murder at will." He shot Bridgette a look. "I'm sorry for your loss, sheriff," he added. "I know you and Maude were very close."

Bridgette nodded. "She was my godmother. I guess her murder means four innocents are dead, plus Moss. That's the largest body count Clinton County has seen in a single day ever."

I stood up from the couch.

"The good news," I said, "is that Sweet is alive. And so long as he's alive, I think we can use him to put an end to whoever is doing the killing."

D'Amico focused in on me. "You got a theory about who's doing the killing?"

"Isn't it obvious, trooper man?" I said.

He rolled his eyes.

"Sure it is," he said. "I just want to hear it from your mouth."

D'Amico was smarter than I thought. Maybe he'd even suspected something less than kosher going down inside the bowels of Dannemora Prison for some time now. But as a state policeman, his number one priority was the apprehension of the two cons. An investigation into wrongdoings at the prison would be the responsibility of the local police and Sheriff Hylton. At least at the outset. It would also be the responsibility of those two FBI agents who'd been sneaking around, and threatening a federal takeover of the escaped con investigation.

But as for me, I had a job to do. Valente hired me to find Sweet and

Moss before D'Amico did, and deliver the two cons to his doorstep. My first screw up came in the form of a dead Reginald Moss. I was now facing my second screw up, which was delivering Sweet to the Clinton County Jail, when I should have just kept driving south to Albany. But then there was his hand. The fact that he was still bleeding. That gangrene could set in at any time. Chances were, if I carted him to Albany, he'd eventually go into shock, followed by death.

But now I had to make the best of an all-around bad situation, and for me that meant using Sweet to expose whatever the hell was truly going on inside the Crypt, and who it involved, which, at this point, was more than likely the governor of the Empire State.

"Listen, D'Amico," I said, "the only thing Sweet wants more than a new right hand is to get free of this place. He goes back to prison or he's delivered to Governor Valente down in Albany, he's as good as dead."

The trooper blinked, shook his head.

"You trying to tell me that what's happening inside the prison… the attack that just occurred inside this jail…is somehow related to the fucking governor?"

Blood crossed his arms over his chest. "That exactly what he trying to tell you, shorty."

That was when I poured myself another shot, and that was when I proceeded to recount for D'Amico everything that Sweet told me about the drug trafficking and child pornography ring being operated not only in the depths of Dannemora Prison, but potentially in dozens of maximum security pens all across this great country of ours. And just to add backup to the words I so eloquently enunciated for the little guy, I pulled out my smartphone, thumbed the record app, then pressed Play.

As I suspected, D'Amico proved himself an attentive audience.

"Gentlemen and lady," he said after a long beat. "What we have here is a criminal conspiracy of Biblical proportions."

CHAPTER 36

The normally stoic, if not rock hard face on the state trooper took on a decidedly soft patina. It wasn't the truth about the system that was hurting him, so much as the now destroyed faith in his fellow law enforcement brothers and sisters in arms that had him so down. Or so I could only assume. His gait slow and pessimistic, he walked the few steps to Bridgette's desk.

"You got an extra one of those Dixie cups?" he said somewhat under his breath.

She opened a drawer, retrieved one, handed it to him from across the desk. Then, she grabbed hold of the bottle neck, set that down hard onto the desk. He poured himself a shot. A double. Then drank it down in one swift swallow.

He set the cup back down slowly, contemplatively, so that the only sound in the square office was the empty, hollow ring of the Dixie cup when its rigid waxed bottom rim connected with the hard wood desk. He nodded, as though answering a question he silently posed for himself.

"You're gonna need another bottle of whiskey soon," he said. Then, taking a step back, as if to address us all, "We're also going to require a smokescreen. Some kind of story we can make up to keep the press gathered outside this jail and Dannemora Prison from revealing the truth. That Moss is dead and Sweet is incarcerated."

"And that a team of corrections officers led by Rodney Pappas killed Joyce and Mean Gene."

"That too," D'Amico said. "We need some real medical help for Sweet. Also, those three bodies are going to start to smell unless we get them down to the morgue."

"I'll take care of that," Bridgette said. "Forensics will need to sweep them. Christ, I haven't even called the coroner." She shook her head. "Who knows what the press is reporting? They must have heard the gunshots."

"They used sound suppressors inside a reinforced concrete block jail," I said. "Those little pops could be heard all the way out front, but they didn't alarm anyone. What alarmed them was Mr. D'Amico's cavalry."

"Somebody's got to act like a real officer of the law around here," the trooper said.

"What are you going to do about the prison? The Crypt?" Bridgette said to D'Amico. "An army of FBI agents is about to come down on Dannemora, and when that happens, all bets are off."

I set my Dixie cup down on the desk beside D'Amico's. I shot a glance at Blood. The wink of his right eye told me he knew what I was about to say before I said it.

"I wanna go in," I said. "I wanna go in with Blood, and I want to do it ASAP if not sooner."

Feigning a crooked expression, D'Amico looked at me like I was crazy.

"And how do you propose to do that?" he said. "You can't just walk through the front door, ask the guard sergeant to see the Crypt."

"You're right, D'Amico," I said. "But we can take Sweet up on his offer to break *back* inside the prison under the guise of his stealing our three hundred Gs in exchange for his freedom."

D'Amico walked back to the desk, poured another shot, drank it down. "You're going to break into prison. Usually doesn't work that way."

"How hard can it be?" said Blood. "COs always focused on cons trying to get out. Means they won't be looking for cons to get back in."

"Still going to take some skill, and some trust in a man who not only killed a cop, but ran him over with Ford F150 twenty times."

"You think he knows a way back into the joint?" D'Amico said.

"Again, it's all about the trust. Depends on who he trusts on the inside to let him back in, and if that trust is reciprocal."

"Sounds complicated," Blood said. "Like a relationship."

"That's why you choose to be single, Blood, my brother," I said.

"That's why any woman who gets involved with you eventually choose to be single."

My eyes automatically shifted to Bridgette's. She caught my gaze, read my mind, cleared her throat. I knew she wanted to change the subject like some people want to change radio stations. She stood up.

"I'm going to prepare a statement for the press," she said. "In the meantime, I'll make sure Karla contacts a doctor and that we get Sweet fixed up as good as possible for whatever it is you're all going to face inside Dannemora and down inside the Crypt."

"Oh, and we'll need something else too," Blood said, uncrossing his arms.

"What's that?" Bridgette said, grabbing hold of the door knob, turning to him.

"More bullets. Lots of them."

CHAPTER 37

While a local doctor sewed Sweet back up inside his small cell and pumped him up with enough antibiotic to make his veins glow, Bridgette prepared a short statement which she delivered to the press outside the front glass doors of the sheriff's office. The briefing centered around an area of Adirondack real estate fifteen miles to the east of Dannemora and Plattsburgh called Willsboro. A mountainous rural area occupied by a scattering of two thousand inhabitants, plus numerous hunting cabins and even a deer preserve maintained by a hunting collective, the members of which lived and worked in New York City, but who made the drive up north on the weekends in their big black Suburban SUVs to be one with the land.

According to Bridgette, the two convicts were spotted in the area by a local resident only this morning, and that the investigation was now going to shift to a five-by-five square mile of land in Willsboro center. When one reporter raised his hand, inquired as to the reason behind the raucous noise that could be heard coming from out of the depths of the jail earlier, Bridgette thought quick. "That was nothing more than a training exercise. Make no mistakes, people, all rumors of an escape attempt on behalf of Gene Bender and Joyce Mathews are unfounded." She failed to mention Larry Mathews, but then his arrest and murder hadn't yet been made public. She then thanked the crowd and despite the dozen questions lobbed at her all at once, she quickly escaped by heading back into the office through the front glass doors.

But two or three minutes didn't pass before the gang of journalists jumped back in their vans, cars, and mobile broadcasting vehicles and began heading straight for Willsboro. Clearly, the ruse worked. Now, while the press was focused on another area of Upstate New York, Blood and I could find a way to get back inside the prison without being spotted by dozens of pairs of prying eyes and cameras.

Convening once more into Bridgette's office, Sweet was brought inside. Vincent D'Amico was also present. Sweet's right hand was now tightly bandaged and there was a small spot of rust colored blood that formed on the area where his thumb used to be.

"Here's the deal," D'Amico said. "You're going back to Dannemora."

Sweet's eyes went wide. I thought he was going to throw up.

"You can't fucking do that to me," he said. "I go back to that prison today, I won't live to see the morning." His eyes watered. "You hear me, sheriff? You've just signed off on my execution."

Bridgette sat behind the desk looking very official and stern.

"I'm sorry, Derrick," she said, "but the law is the law and we have no choice. If it's any consolation, you'll spend the next week or two in the prison infirmary. You'll be provided with your own personal corrections officer bodyguard. One of those big muscle heads who works inside Rodney's personal circle. You have nothing to worry about."

Sweet was already pale. His skin turned even more white at the mention of Rodney. For a split second, I thought his heart might give out. Bridgette glanced at me quickly. She knew that I knew she was really pouring it on.

"But I thought the governor was taking responsibility for me."

"The governor agrees," Bridgette said. "You're to go straight back to prison. Do not stop on Go, do not collect two hundred bucks."

Now the tears that had been precariously balanced around the fleshy rims of his eyes started overflowing. Sweet even fell out of his chair, onto his knees. He lifted up both his hands, pressed them together like he was praying for divine intervention on his behalf. The good hand joined to the heavily bandaged bad hand made him look like a casualty of war...a prisoner of war.

"Please, sheriff," he cried, "I'm begging you. Please don't put me back there in that iron house. I won't live to see the sunrise tomorrow morning."

Blood leaned into me. "He either a real good actor, or he really scared shitless."

"I hope, in fact, he doesn't shit himself," I whispered back.

I stole a peek at D'Amico standing by the door on the opposite side of the room. He was biting down on his bottom lip. As if to answer Blood's question, I got the feeling he interpreted Sweet's dismay not as an act, but real fear oozing from a man who clearly feared his own imminent death.

"For reasons of keeping your capture a secret and away from the prying eyes of a starving media," D'Amico said, "we've arranged for Mr. Marconi and Mr. Blood here to provide your transportation back to the prison."

Sweet, still down on his knees, turned his head, focused his eyes on the trooper. He stood up slowly, his mouth open, lower jaw hanging down by his slippered feet.

"Are you fucking kidding?" he said. "These two jerks work for Governor Valente. They'll kill me first chance they get, just like they killed Picasso."

"Valente fired us," I lied. "And I didn't kill Moss. He killed himself when he tried to kill me first. *Capisce*?"

"Gospel," Blood chimed in.

"Now don't you worry, Mr. Sweet," D'Amico said. "Me and my men will be following you every step of the way." Cocking his head over his shoulder. "At a safe enough distance, naturally."

"Oh, now I feel a hell of a lot better," Sweet said. Then, looking up at the ceiling, "Sweet Jesus, I'm gonna die."

Bridgette got up, came around the desk, slapped a cuff onto Sweet's good hand, and then placed the other cuff around Blood's wrist.

"Good Christ," Sweet barked, "anyone but Black Tonto."

"Hey," Blood said while the metal cuff was attached to his wrist, "I take offense to that."

Sweet peered up at Blood. He was genuinely afraid of the big ebony man. And I couldn't blame him one bit.

"If that's all, gentlemen and lady," D'Amico said, "let's get this show on the road."

I went for the door just as the trooper opened it.

"If this doesn't work," he whispered under his breath, "I lose my job and my pension."

"Don't worry," I said, "it'll work."

Behind me, Bridgette tossed Blood the key to the cuffs before exiting the room. Then came Derrick Sweet, the scared-of-his-own-shadow fugitive from justice being dragged by the wrist.

"Dead man walking," he said under his breath. "That's what I am. Stupid dead asshole walking."

CHAPTER 38

The object that had been blocking the cell bay's rear exit had finally been removed and the three of us piled back into my old 4Runner. Blood and Sweet took the back seat while I fired up the recently refurbished eight cylinder and waited for the backyard gates to slide open. When they did, I slowly drove on out, careful not to raise the suspicions of any of the few remaining reporters stubbornly clung to the county lockup hoping for a major scoop.

Only when we were far enough away from the sheriff's office and heading towards Dannemora, the narrow country road flanked on both sides by tall trees and thick brush, did I ask Blood to remove Sweet's cuff.

I watched Sweet in the rearview mirror. His expression was one of confusion.

"What gives?" he said. "Thought you guys were responsible for me."

"You still want your freedom?" I said.

The confused expression turned into a smile. "Fuck yeah."

Blood gave him a slight elbow. "It'll cost you, thin man. But not the three hundred you originally offered."

Blood, raising the ante. Wish I'd thought of that myself...

"How much?" Sweet said.

"Five hundred," Blood said. "Two fifty a piece."

The con bit down on his lips and rubbed his damaged hand.

"Fucking choice do I have?" he said. "Let's hope that kind of cash is sitting around the Crypt and that Rodney himself isn't sitting on it."

"No choice," Blood said.

Up ahead in the distance now, the big, razor wire-topped walls of Dannemora Prison. From my vantage point, it looked like most of the journos and reporters who'd planted themselves here over the past couple of days had now transported themselves to Willsboro. Looked like the media was taking Sheriff Hylton's presser very seriously. A good thing, you asked me. The less eyes on us, the better.

"Home sweet home," I said.

"Think I'm gonna puke," Sweet said.

"Ain't life grand?" Blood said.

I pulled off the side of the road, asked Sweet the best place for me to pull in.

"Service entrance," he said. "You're gonna see a guard shack out front, of course. An armed guard there. But if it's the right screw, he'll know me. Could be we'll be okay."

"What's 'could be' mean?" Blood said.

"Means if he knows me, and he don't hate me, he'll let me pass after I explain the situation to him. Course, you'll have to pay him."

"You mean *you'll* have to pay him," I said.

"Whatever the fuck," he said dismissively. "I probably won't live through the afternoon anyway."

"And what happens when he let us through?" Blood said. "We just walk in the back door, shout, 'Home again, home again, jiggety-jig'?"

"Not exactly," he said. "My best bet is to go in through the laundry detail. You probably already know this, Marconi, but there's a steady stream of clean linens going in, and shit-stained stuff coming out. I go in with the clean, and out with the shit. That is, I'm still alive."

"What's with the I?" I said.

"Yeah," Blood said. "There no I in team. Only an E, as in we."

"Wait a minute," Sweet said, "you can't come in there with me. Rodney and his inner circle of evil maggots want me dead. Maybe I can get myself in if I promise the right payoffs to the right individuals, but they'll kill me on the spot they see me sneaking back into prison with a couple of armed soldiers of fortune."

"That what we are, Blood?" I said. "Soldiers of fortune?"

"More like soldiers of *mis*fortune. A regular dirty duo, partner." Then to Sweet, "No choice. We coming for the ride."

"Then I want a weapon. At least do me that favor."

"You crazier than I thought," Blood said. "You don't get to play with guns no more."

"Then no deal."

"Keep, get Governor Valente on the phone. Tell him we're ready to bring in our prisoner."

Sweet put both hands up in surrender. "Okay, okay, fuck, fuck, fucking fuck. Let's just go. See what happens."

"That's the spirit," I said.

I threw the tranny back in drive, pulled back out onto the road to perdition.

CHAPTER 39

The service entrance to the prison was located in a wooded area maybe a full half mile away from the general prison entrance, which was situated in the center of town. Like Sweet said, there was a guard shack manned by a single CO. Thank God for rampant prison understaffing. Before you could reach the guard shack, you had to stop before a formidable gate that belonged to the much larger razor wire-topped perimeter fence surrounding the entire prison facility. I pulled up to the gates and waited, knowing that the fire engine red Toyota was being filmed by at least several different closed circuit TV monitors and that it was quite possible several black and yellow New York State Corrections vehicles might pull up behind me, flashers flashing, armed COs jumping out, weapons pointed at our heads.

But that didn't happen. Instead, Sweet rolled down the window and *allowed* himself to be seen.

"Sure that's a good idea?" I said.

"Those cameras up there," he said, nodding to the CCTV camera mounted to both the exterior of the guard shack and the fence itself. "They're dummies. Some of them anyway. Prison security budget always in the red. Most people don't know that, or it would scare the hell of them."

"You sure about that?" Blood added. "About the dummy cameras, I mean. Don't seem real to me. That shit real to you, Keep?"

I cocked my head over my shoulder.

"Doesn't seem unreal either," I said. "Sweet's right. Max prisons always run in the red. You cut where you can."

"Sure as shit," Sweet said. "Super's orders. He's all about balancing the budget. On the surface that is. But underneath it all, he's got another agenda. You see, Mr. Blood, this service entrance is the Silk fucking Road. The main route for transporting contraband inside the joint, and the main road for bringing shit out. Every prison and jail, from minimum security to the most hard-ass super max, has got one."

So that seals it, then. Clark is as filthy as they come.

"So why go to all the trouble of escaping through a waste pipe?" I said.

"It's not allowed. There'd be no faster way to shut the Silk Road down than by allowing a prisoner or two to escape every once in a while." He shoots a look at me. "Believe me, a few have tried and had their brains blown out because of it. Shit like that doesn't get in the news because their deaths are always reported as prisoner on prisoner violence, or maybe the result of a bad accident. Usually, the bodies are cremated before a medical examiner can get at them."

"The COs," I said. "Men like Rodney. They run the Silk Road."

Sweet nodded.

"Very good, Mr. Marconi. And Clark is the big boss man. The Ayatollah of rock 'n'rolla. They run the Silk Road, control what's imported and exported. They're all about quality control."

The burly guard stepped out of the shack. He was a clean shaven black man, dressed in corrections officer black military style clothing. He had an M16 strapped over his shoulder. He was also wearing a sidearm in a holster strapped to his left thigh. His eyes were shielded by a pair of aviator sunglasses.

"And that screw staring us down," I said, cocking my head over my right shoulder, "he's an employee of the Silk Road?"

"Yup," said Sweet. "He damn well is, which is why I let him see me. Because when you work on the Silk Road, you take care of yourself first. That means you can be bought." He worked up a wad of mucous, spit it out the window. "You guys are lucky. This screw knows me. He'll work with me. If it had been anybody else, you'd be reversing the hell out of here, pedal to the motherfuckin' metal."

"The screws can be bought," I said. "But not enough to traffic prisoners in and out." It was a question.

"Listen, this guy might let us *entre vous* in exchange for some sweet dough-rei-mi," Sweet said, "but no way in hell he about to let us back out. Therein lies our ultimate problemo."

"So what you telling us," Blood said, "is we entering the lion's den and the den ain't got no exit."

"I'm sorry," Sweet said, "you must have been counting on a nice little picnic." The iron gate slowly opened. "Still sure you wanna do this, gentlemen?"

In answer his question, I pulled forward.

"Fun begins now," I said.

The gate closed behind us. When the metal struck metal, the solid noise made my stomach muscles tighten, my pulse pump faster. I rolled down my window.

"Good afternoon, officer," I said. "We're making a delivery."

Glancing in the rearview, I saw Sweet's face grow taught. It also went chalky and pale again.

"How's it hanging, Lucas?" Sweet said, his Adam's apple bobbing up and down with each syllable uttered.

"Derrick Sweet," Lucas said, not without a smile and a shake of his head. "I always knew you were a dumb shit. But who the hell tries to sneak back inside a prison once they've already busted out?" He laughed. "You forget your wallet or something?"

Sweet smiled.

"Something like that, Lucas." Then, "These men are my friends. They're gonna wait while I do what I gotta do. There's some pretty green in it for you."

"How much?"

"Name a price."

Lucas thought it over for a few seconds.

"Ten K. Non-negotiable," he said.

Sweet shook his head.

"Give me a fucking break, Lucas," he said. "I got a better chance of crawling back up my mother's vagina than I do of nabbing that much cash."

Good Christ, we're parked outside the prison and these two numb nuts are negotiating...

But here's the deal: no way I was going to allow Sweet to confiscate even one dollar of that cash inside the Crypt. That is, the cash existed in the first place. But if it did, it would be state's evidence, and you didn't fuck with state's evidence unless you had a very good reason. What all of this meant, of course, was that I had to do something. Something quick or this thing would be all blown to hell before it even started. I pulled out my .45, pointed it at Lucas the guard.

"Down on your knees and lose the fucking gun before you get down there."

He hesitated.

"Do it," I said, thumbing back the hammer on the already chambered round.

"Fuck you doing?" Sweet said. His voice sounded like there were marbles stuck in his throat.

Blood knew precisely what I was doing. That was why he opened the glove box, pulled out the roll of duct tape that I stored inside it to utilize as a poor man's handcuffs. Opening the door, he slipped out, went around the front of the vehicle. Crouching down, he picked up the M16 that was now set on the ground, handed it to me through the open window.

"That make up for the one you lost down in the shelter," he said. He then grabbed hold of the CO's shirt collar, pulled him back into the guard shack, proceeded to tape up his wrists and ankles. He also ripped off a piece of tape and covered the screw's big mouth. Before exiting the shack, he depressed some select keys on the laptop, killing the CCTV monitors. The ones that were connected to working cameras anyway. I could only wonder if killing them meant we would be tripping a general alarm or, conversely, that nothing would happen at all.

I took a good look at Sweet's face in the rearview mirror. Even from where I was sitting, I could see the beads of sweat that formed on his brow. A few of my own sweat beads had no doubt formed on my own forehead. Blood came back around, got back in the 4Runner.

"Go," he said.

I pulled ahead, along the Silk Road.

CHAPTER 40

I parked beside a big white laundry truck, killed the engine.

Sweet opened the back door.

"Follow me," he said. "And try not to talk."

We exited the 4Runner and gathered just outside the back cargo bay of the laundry truck. When the coast was clear, Sweet waved us on with a hand signal.

"Inside the truck," he said. "Choose a bin, climb inside. Cover yourself up with the linens."

I peeked inside the truck's open cargo bay. There were maybe a dozen big aluminum bins set on pallets positioned one beside the other. Maybe half the bins had already been unloaded, leaving six to choose from. Without speaking, we all chose a bin and jumped inside, covering ourselves up with the fresh white linens. Within a few seconds, I could make out the mechanized motor of a forklift come to retrieve more bins.

One by one, the forklift carted us inside a big echo-chamber of a laundry facility. It was hot, steamy, and loud. At one point, I managed to peek out from under the linens. The room was filled with men dressed in white jumpers. They were feeding the big machines with soiled clothing, underwear, socks, and towels. Apparently, the only items to be cleaned and pressed at a separate off-site facility were the bed linens. Scanning the place, I made out only one corrections officer. He was standing at the far end of the large room. He was staring at the screen on his smartphone.

I ducked back down inside and waited for the forklift to stop and set the bin down. When it did, I listened for the sound of the machine moving away from me. That was when I popped my head out from under the linens, saw that no one was eyeing me, and jumped out of the bin.

Out the corner of my eye, I saw Blood and Sweet. They were crouched down behind their respective aluminum bins. I, too, crouched down.

"What now?" I whispered.

Sweet cocked his head in the direction of a plain wall to which a metal panel was attached. At first I didn't know what he was doing until I saw him slowly stand, look one way and then the other. When he opened the panel, he placed his index finger pad onto what appeared to be a square, glass digital scanner. The glass flashed when the scanner was activated.

What was this place? Something out of a science fiction movie?

A door that was flush with the wall opened then. Sweet raised his arm, issued us a wave that told us to follow him through the open door, and into an empty corridor.

"Through there," he said, closing the door behind us and pointing to the solid metal door that blocked the end of the narrow passage.

We jogged our way to the door. He opened it, closed it behind him. The door not only slammed against the solid metal frame, three dead bolts electronically engaged. Turning, I faced an empty concrete room that facilitated two big stainless steel cargo elevator doors.

"This is where things get tricky," Sweet said. "They got cameras all over the place. And unlike the guard shack out on the Silk Road, all of them are operational. Chances are we'll meet some resistance when we make it to the bottom. But there's no other way inside. Unless, that is, we go back outside and around to the back of the building. But even then, we'd have to find a way to break through a deadbolted metal door."

I drew my .45 and Blood drew his 9mm.

"Got an extra one of those?" Sweet said.

"Just stay close," I said.

He hit the down button on the elevator panel. A beat later, the doors slid open. We stepped inside, not knowing what the hell to expect.

CHAPTER 41

The ride down was longer than I might have expected. I guessed we'd travelled at least ten stories underground. Nothing like this existed when I was running Green Haven. Or if it did, I was completely unaware of it. One thing was for sure, the people who built the Crypt weren't kidding around. This was a sophisticated operation, and expensive.

During the ride, Sweet explained that where we were going was originally constructed back in the late 1970s as a bomb shelter for New York's most distinguished politicians, like the governor for instance, should the Russians and the US unleash their nuclear arsenals at one another. Thus the high-tech gadgetry up in the laundry facility. But in the years since the Cold War ended, the space had been transformed into something else entirely.

"What you're about to see will probably shock the living crap out of you," he said. "Some of it might even make you sick. But like my mother used to say, Mr. Blood and Mr. Marconi, it is what it is."

"That what she say after you run that sheriff's deputy over with your truck a hundred times?" Blood said.

"Actually, Mr. Blood," he said, "she thought the prick had it coming."

"Your poor mother," I said.

"Ain't that the truth," Blood said.

The doors opened.

"Gentlemen," the ex-con said, "behold, the Crypt."

Luck was on our side. Because the long, brightly lit corridor we faced was empty. But that didn't mean we were alone. At least judging from the scattered voices belonging to the handful of men shouting out orders from behind closed doors. I could also make out something else. The high-pitched wail that I'd heard up in Clark's office. But this time, the wail was much louder.

"Hell is that?" I said.

"Come with me," Sweet said.

We followed him out of the elevator and into the hall. The first set of metal doors on the right were identified by the word *DORMITORY* in solid white letters. I peeked in through the chicken-wire safety glass panel that was embedded into the solid metal door. There were several sets of metal bunk beds taking up floor space inside the otherwise empty room. Several kids were sleeping on the beds. Others were sitting up. It took me a few seconds for the reality to sink in, but all the kids were chained to the metal framed bunkbeds. They were dressed in blaze orange jumpers, just like the ones ISIS forces its prisoners to wear. Some of the kids were despondent, crying, weeping, wailing.

"Jesus," I said. "Slaves. The kids are slaves."

"I say we break them out now," Blood said. There was acid in his tone. I could feel the anger radiating off of him.

"We need to keep moving," Sweet said. "We get into the office, I can access the vault. But we're exposed out here."

"He's right," I said. "You two go. Get working on the access code. We'll deal with the kids on our way out."

Although I didn't come right out and say it, I wasn't leaving the Crypt without those kids. For certain, Blood knew my intention without my having to spell it out. He could read my mind. Sometimes, I could read his. We were in sync that way. But for now...right that very minute...my overriding objective was to make a photographic record of the place that I could use against Clark, against Rodney, against Valente. My purpose was clear. I was to gather up enough evidence to shut this place and others like it down, then bring those responsible for it, to justice.

Blood and Sweet proceeded to move on down the corridor. I pulled out my smartphone, went to the pictures app, snapped several photos of the kids through the glass. I made a three-hundred-sixty-degree spin on the balls of my feet, snapping photos of the underground corridor. Moving on, I shifted to the opposite side of the corridor, to a place marked *WAREHOUSE*. Inside the glass I made out stacks of boxes set on palates and wrapped in transparent plastic. The boxes were marked *Pickles*. But I knew without having to tear a box open that they contained product. Drug product. The Crypt housed a meth lab. The boxes were filled with dope.

Sweet and Blood were almost at the other end of the corridor by the time I arrived at the next metal door. Peering inside the door's safety glass pane, I saw a wide open room that housed a sophisticated air filtration system, several stainless steel tanks for boiling large quantities of material, plus driers and drying racks, like the kind you might find in an industrial sized bakery. Several men dressed in white HEPA suits and sporting oxygen masks over their faces were working inside the facility. You didn't have to be a genius to know they were cooking meth and doing so in large proportions. My camera pointed at the operation through the glass, I snapped away.

I then made my way quickly back across the floor once more. This time I came face to face with a small kitchen and dining area. Beside that was a studio for filming movies. Without doubt, the porn and snuff movies Sweet described. The room supported portable lighting and filming equipment, plus a stage consisting of a plain table outfitted with chains and iron shackles. A drain had been installed in the center of the concrete floor. It made me sick to my stomach.

I tried the door. It opened. The interior of the television studio-like room was covered in exposed wires and other electronic gear. Another table with several laptops set up on it had been situated near a far windowless wall. I sat before one of the laptops, depressed the enter button, bringing up the home screen. I found a listing of maybe two dozen movies. I glanced through the list of titles, all of which appeared to be borrowed by the video actor's first names. One of them that caught my eye was titled *Moss + Lisa + Jeremey*. I clicked on it. The *50 Shades of Grey* table with its chains came into view. Suddenly two kids entered into the picture. A girl and a boy, no more than twelve or thirteen years old. They were thin. Malnourished. Then a man came into view. Reginald Moss. He looked like a giant compared to the far smaller kids. He began to undress in front of them and then they began to do things to him.

Instinctively, I turned, faced the floor, and vomited.

When I was emptied, I slapped the laptop cover closed and stood up. Grabbing hold of the laptop with both hands, I tossed it against the concrete block wall. It shattered into a dozen pieces.

"You fuckers," I said aloud, as if the bastards responsible for the horrors taking place down here could hear me. It felt good to say it anyway. Retrieving my phone once more, I took a dozen pictures of the studio. Before I left the room, I approached the shattered computer and retrieved the memory card from the broken keyboard housing, stuffed it into my cargo pants pocket. Then I made my way back into the corridor.

I located the vault which was housed inside a room accessed by yet another metal door. And beside that was the office space. A space that also contained an inordinate amount of semi-automatic and automatic weapons both long and short. I took pictures of it all, documented almost every square foot of the space not only for Sheriff Hylton and Trooper D'Amico to see, but also for the world to see. But before any of that, I needed to send the photos on to someone who would appreciate their value more than anyone else.

Governor Valente.

Selecting a series of twenty separate photos, I then forwarded a mass MMS to the governor. Only when that was accomplished did I send the photos onto both Bridgette and D'Amico. For good measure,

I CC'd FBI Agents Muscolino and Doyle. For certain my location ten stories underground would prohibit the transmission from taking place right away, but the photos would go out as soon as I was back in WiFi range.

The door to the office was open. There were several metal desks set up one beside the other on the floor, just like you would find in the general booking area of a police station. To my right was the wall of weapons. To my left were shelves that contained boxes of ammo. The wall behind the desks was constructed of plain concrete, except for a narrow area at the far end that contained a metal door with no glass embedded inside it. The ceiling-mounted lighting was LED and bathed us in a warm white glow.

Sweet was rummaging through the desk drawers, searching for something. I pulled out my .45, thumbed back the hammer, aimed the barrel at his face.

He threw his hands up in the air. "What the fuck, man?"

"Keeper," Blood said, "what you doing?"

"That studio," I said. "I saw what kind of movies they make in there. Saw one with your partner, Moss, as the headlining star."

He swallowed, his Adam's apple bobbing up and down in his skinny chicken neck.

"Tell me you never made one of those movies," I went on. "Tell me now, because otherwise, I'm gonna blast your brains all over the wall."

"Take it easy, Keep," Blood said, "we need his nervous skinny ass for now."

"Tell me, Sweet!" I shouted.

His face had gone pale again, the bandage on his damaged hand stained with fresh blood.

"I know you don't trust me and you probably won't believe me when I tell you I never once made one of those movies, nor did I ever touch one of those kids. My job down here was computers. I'm fucking IT. A computer geek and an asshole, remember?"

"You're right," I said, "I don't believe you."

"But you have to," he said. "Listen, physically speaking, Moss was far better outfitted for the job."

"You mean he was hung," Blood said.

"For lack of a better term," Sweet said. "Yes. And if it makes you feel any better at all, Keeper, Moss was forced into doing those films. Forced at gunpoint. He didn't perform, they would have shot him in the back of the head inside his cell and burned his body in the furnace. You understand what I'm saying?"

"Keeper," Blood said. "Stand down. He telling the truth. Let's focus on the job and get the hell out of here."

Thumbing the hammer back to the safety position, I turned away from Sweet, wiped the tears from my eyes with the backs of my hand.

Moments later, Sweet was back to searching for the vault code.

"Fuck, shit, fuck!" he barked. "I can't find the fucking code anywhere."

"You don't remember it?" Blood said, his 9mm still gripped in his right, shooting hand.

"It changes daily," Sweet said. "And even then, only Rodney and the super are in possession of it. Only way I'd know is if they asked me to use it."

He pulled up the top on one of the computers and sat down on the chair.

Sweet then said, "There is a possibility, however, that I might be able to hack my way into the code."

"You the computer expert," Blood said.

I looked at Blood. He looked back at me. I knew what he was thinking. We already had the photos and proof we needed to prove to the world that the Crypt inside Dannemora was being used for trafficking not only little kids as sex slaves, but also for moving meth. What difference did the cash make at this point?

He approached me.

"The money," he said. "We can leave the state's evidence alone and find a way out of here. Or we can take it, and at the same time, throw a real wrench into their operation. Take away their fiduciary leverage."

"Maybe take a little for yourself," I said, not without a smile. Despite the circumstances, it felt good to smile. Felt good to enact our revenge.

"I got a nephew. My sister's boy. He could use it to pay for college one day."

"There's a lot of good things that money can be used for," I said, recalling my vow not to take even a dollar of it if, in fact, it existed. "But you and I both know that we can't do it. It's against the rules, and if we ever want to work again, we need to play by them."

He nodded.

"However," I said, "what if, once we free those poor kids, they manage to find a way to steal the money on their own, stuff their own pockets without our being the least bit aware."

Blood smiled.

"Payback," he said.

"Much deserved payback," I said.

I might have high-fived my partner, had the general alarm not sounded.

CHAPTER 42

"They've fucking breached the crypt!" Warden Clark, screaming. He's pacing behind his big desk, a lit cigarette balanced between trembling lips. The cigarette isn't halfway finished yet, but still he finds himself digging into the pack for another. He stops and stares down at his laptop. "They fucking drove right into the back lot in a fucking bright red Toyota four by four in broad fucking daylight. And it's all because of you, you over-fed, muscle-bound, moron!"

Rodney Pappas stands in the center of the square office, hands by his side clenched into fists, his heart pumping, toxic adrenalin flowing through hot-blooded veins.

"You already got one going," the bald-headed captain of the guard points out.

Clark turns, eyes his subordinate with scorn worthy of a master to his mangy mutt.

"Let me explain something to you, Rodney," he says, lighting the *new cigarette off the old one.* "If those three men were able to break into the prison so easily, it's because your men let it happen. Your men can obviously be easily bought."

Rodney smiles.

"That's rich," *he says.* "Look who's talking,"

"Excuse me?" *Clark snaps.*

"You, too, can be easily bought. Or else you wouldn't have agreed to run the operations down in the Crypt. You would have walked away from it. Walked away from the Silk Road, walked away from Little Siberia altogether. You would have looked for a more honest line of work. But instead, you saw green. Lots of it. We all did. So own up to your own low moral standing before casting a stupid ass judgement on a lowlife member of your support staff like myself."

"You know what they want, don't you?" *Clark says.*

"No, what do they want?"

"They want the money in the vault. That's the only reason a fuckup like Sweet would risk breaking back into a prison he already broke out of."

"The cocksucker was already scheduled to come back. Blood and Marconi were to take care of the delivery under the blind eyes of the press. That's what we arranged with Sheriff Hylton. But instead they pulled a fast one, and broke in through the laundry instead."

"You dumb shit," *Clark barks.* "You don't think Hylton and D'Amico aren't aware of your little military operation inside their own jail? You think they don't know it was you who killed those three key witnesses in cold blood?"

Rodney swallows something cold, hard, and bitter. "We wore masks. They didn't get a positive ID, but they did manage to shoot one of my men in the thigh."

Clark sucks on his cigarette so fiercely, half of it burns down to gray ash.

"You're dumber than I thought," he says.

Rodney feels the veins popping out of his tree trunk neck.

"When this is over," he whispers, "I'm gonna rip your head off and piss down your neck."

"What did you just say, Corrections Officer Pappas?"

Rodney clears his throat. "I said, this thing isn't quite a total train wreck."

"We literally opened the doors for Marconi to bring Sweet back in according to SOP, only to be stabbed in the back."

"Look it, Mr. Clark. I agree that Sweet wants money. He was an integral part of our organization. He and Moss, may the devil never let his soul rest. If anyone knows how to breach the prison and breach the vault, it's him. But I think Marconi and Blood want more. They're good people. Moral people. I think their intention is to expose the Crypt for what it is. And expose you and me in the process. Just like Gene, Joyce, and Larry would have done if I...we... allowed them to live."

Clark approaches the window, stares outside at the late afternoon sunshine.

"So what the fuck are you going to do to protect the Crypt, myself, yourself, and the two dozen COs and lab civilians working inside it?"

"I'm already working on it," Rodney says, lifting up his left hand, taking a glance at the time. "It's three forty-five now. Trust me when I say that Derrick Sweet, Keeper Marconi, and that mountain of a coon, Blood, will not live to see the clock strike four."

CHAPTER 43

The alarm blared.

Sweet looked up from the computer.

"Holy shit," he said. "We're busted."

"You got the code?" I barked.

"I'm fucking working on it."

"Keep working on it. Blood and I will hold them back."

I went for the gun rack. Without my having to ask, Blood sprinted across the room for the ammo. I pulled an M16 from off the rack, tossed it to my partner as he made his way back to me, then took one down for me. I thought about locking the door, taking defensive positions behind it, but I knew it would be important to hold them back as soon as they stepped off the elevator. Make our defense our best offense.

"Got it!" Sweet shouted.

I looked at him over my shoulder. "You open the vault. We'll take care of the screws. Go now!"

The elevator doors opened up. Both of them. It was like a mad rush of adult-sized, black-clad GI Joe figurines. All of them armed to the teeth, all of them shooting from the hip.

"You go left, I go right!" I shouted.

Blood and I both fired, the rounds connecting with the first wave of COs, dropping them on the spot. Out the corner of my eyes, I saw Sweet open the door to the vault room. Then, I saw him enter inside, raise up his hand to enter a numeric code into the wall-mounted keypad.

The bullets whizzed by my ears. The rounds connected with the solid block wall behind me, ricocheting and pinging off the metal door frames. I returned fire until I was out, then quickly ejected the empty magazine and slammed home a full one. Aim. Fire. Repeat. That was all we had to do.

And then, just like that, no more on-the-take COs.

But we were still taking gunfire. It wasn't coming from the elevators. It was coming from the now shattered window on the meth lab door.

I turned to Blood. "Think we can take them out?"

"How hard can it be? They not fighters. They lab rats."

"That gives me an idea."

I lunged across the corridor, pressed my back up against the wall. Blood followed. The shooters were still trying to hit us, but they couldn't manage to connect with anything other than concrete block wall while firing their weapons through an opening barely larger than a laptop computer screen. Sliding my way over to the door, I was only inches from two separate barrels that stuck out of the broken glass. Maneuvering my M16 so that my left hand held the grip, the thumb on the trigger, and the right hand now holding the forward grip, I shoved the barrel into the broken glass opening and fired at random.

First came the screams and then came the explosion that blew the door off the room

From down on the floor, my back now pressed up against the opposite wall, I looked for Blood. He was also pushed up against the opposite wall, his body, like mine, having been propelled by the force of the explosion. I couldn't be sure, but it was entirely possible that we'd been knocked out for a minute or more.

"You hit?" I said.

He looked down at his legs and belly. Patted himself down.

"Don't think so, Keep. You?"

I performed the same cursory examination. Nothing. Not even a scratch. Miraculously.

"Nada," I said, "but my ears are gonna ring for a while."

"What?" he said. "Can't hear you."

We both stood up, brushed ourselves off. The general alarm had stopped, the electrical supply to it having no doubt been cut off by the blast. The lab was gone. Obliterated. The door and block wall blown entirely out, the lab rats evaporated, or blown to such tiny bits, not much of what remained resembled anything human. All that was left was a pit of mangled metal, jagged concrete, broken gas and severed electrical and water lines.

"Sweet Jesus in heaven," Blood said. "I knew meth was ignitable, but not that unstable and volatile."

"Meth labs blow all the time. All this one needed was a little help."

"Maybe we won the day. They ain't making meth for a while."

But my gut told me that despite winning the battle, the war was far from over.

"More ammo," I said, jogging back into the office. "They're gonna come back at us, and this time, with more fire power."

"True dat," Blood said.

We filled every available pocket with full magazines. On our way back out the door, I grabbed an extra M16, tossed it to Blood. Then I grabbed another for myself.

"From this point on," I said, "we go Rambo on those motherfuckers."

"Nobody fucks with Rambo," Blood said, pulling back the slide on the second automatic rifle.

I slapped a mag into my second M16's housing, racked the slide, switched to full automatic mode. The mechanical noise of two descending cargo elevators filled the damaged corridor.

"Here they come, Blood," I said, now gripping one rifle in one hand, and the second in the other.

Blood raised up his two-fisted M16s. "We end this now."

At the same time the elevator doors slid open, so too did the metal vault door.

The new wave of COs came out shooting. Blood and I opened up on them, cutting them in half at the waist. Like the first time, it was a turkey shoot. They should have learned their lesson from the first go round. But as soon as the first wave was decimated, a second wave of one man per elevator positioned down on one knee clearly came into focus. The M16s they were carrying were armed with grenade launchers.

"Incoming!" I screamed as two live grenades shot straight for us.

CHAPTER 44

I f not for the terrible aim of the two COs launching the grenades, Blood and I would have become a permanent part of the Crypt, our flesh and blood painting the floor, walls, and ceiling. Instinct kicked in and we dropped flat onto our chests as the grenades passed overhead, striking the far wall behind us. We returned the fire, cutting down the last two COs only a split second before the elevator doors closed once more.

We got back up onto our feet, brushed away the shards of concrete and glass from our bodies.

I inhaled and exhaled a hot, sour breath. Then, "You think that's the last of them? There can only be so many on-the-take COs working the Crypt."

"It's not like they can sic all the guards on us," he said. "They do that, they implicate themselves in some serious bad shit."

"That doesn't mean there aren't more coming at us. And when they do, they're likely to pack some tear gas canisters inside those grenade launchers. They can't kill us outright, they'll try to gas us, then kill us." Shifting my focus to the vault. "Sweet, how you making out in there?"

"Come see for yourself!" he yelled.

Blood and I made our way in, and nearly passed out from what we witnessed.

The vault was maybe fifteen feet by fifteen feet. Taking up almost the entirety of the floor space were no less than half a dozen aluminum laundry bins filled with cash.

I turned to Blood. "Rough estimate."

He cocked his head, took a step forward staring into the closest bin. "Large denominations," he said. "Each bundle, maybe three to five million, give or take, depending upon the consistency of the denomination. All told, maybe upwards of thirty million."

My eyes locked on the cash, glowing richly green in the overhead LED lamp light.

"My guess is they won't miss a million or so, should those kids happen to take notice."

"Cops might miss it when they investigate," Blood said. "But then, you and me don't take nothing for ourselves. That way we don't have to lie. Much."

"We gotta keep up appearances, Blood. Do what's right. But those kids deserve something after what they been through. If the FBI questions us, we'll feign ignorance."

"Or, we could blame Sweet."

The con's brow scrunched up. "You let me go when this is all said and done, you can blame me all you want. It will be my pleasure."

There it was again. The high-pitched wailing. The kids, locked in that room. Chained to the beds.

"Jesus," I said, both hands still gripping one M16 apiece. "The kids. We've got to free them before we give this cash another thought."

"Couldn't agree more," Blood said.

Together, we exited the vault and sprinted the length of the battle damaged corridor to the dormitory.

"Stand back," I said, aiming the M16 at the door lever.

I put three rounds into the lever and the deadbolt above it, managing to rip a six-inch gash in the metal door. Raising my leg, I kicked it open and revealed a room filled with maybe twenty early teenage kids.

Their mostly gaunt faces displayed an odd emotional mixture of fear, sadness, anger, desperation, grief, and just plain happiness that someone…someone good…had finally come to rescue them. First things first: we needed a key. We couldn't just start shooting the locks and spraying the room with lead and shattered metal. Not with all these kids around. Blood locked eyes on mine. As usual, he knew exactly what was running through my brain.

"I see some keys in the desk in the office. Sweet can help."

He ran out of the room before I could respond, and returned a minute later with several small keys. He dropped half of them into my palm and kept the other half. Both of us went to work trying them on the locks until it was discovered that I had the master. From that point on, it was just a matter of unlocking each child.

The kids then began to scream not because they were afraid, but because they were finally free. Finally getting out of this place. Placing my fingers under my tongue, I whistled to get everyone's attention.

"Hang on, everybody," I said. "We're not quite done yet. We still have to make it out of the prison and outside the gates. But before we do anything, I don't want you leaving here empty handed." Then, turning to Blood. "Blood, my man, take a quick look in the kitchen. See if there are any bags we might use."

Blood skipped off in the direction of the kitchen which was accessible to the dorm via an interior door. When he returned he was holding piles of plastic supermarket shopping bags in his hands.

"This do the trick, Keep?"

"Damn straight," I said. "Let's get to work."

Handing each child a shopping bag, we made the short hike down the corridor to the vault, then worked like a team stuffing each and every bag. When we were finished I glanced at my watch. The whole money grabbing operation took maybe ten minutes.

That was when Sweet turned to me.

"What about me?" he said. "I'm still planning on spending the rest of my days in beautiful Mexico."

Sweet was a killer. A cop killer at that. A reprehensible human being by all accounts. But he did help us with freeing those kids. He did cooperate in exposing this dungeon of horrors. If he took some of the cash for himself, that was his business. Right was right, but sometimes it was more right when you put your blinders on.

"Do what you gotta do, Sweet," I said. "And we never had this conversation. At this point, I just wanna get those kids out of here. Fast."

I looked around for another way out beside the elevators. Then I remembered the door at the far end of the office.

"That door," I said to Sweet as he was filling a shopping bag with cash. "Will it lead us out of here?"

"It leads directly to the exterior of the laundry," he said. "But you're going to have to blow your way through the locks. You're not going to find keys for them like you did the padlocks on those kids."

"We've got more ammo than we need."

I was just about ready to gather up the kids and escort them to the door inside the office when the mechanical noise of descending elevators once again filled the corridor.

CHAPTER 45

"Everyone back inside the room!" I shouted. "Close the door and jump back up on your beds. Make it look like you're still locked to the bedframes." Out the corner of my eyes, I spotted a girl of thirteen or fourteen who started to cry. "And don't worry, I'll be back for you. Without fail, I will be back." My eyes went from Sweet and Blood to the elevator doors and back again. "Sweet," I said, "grab yourself a weapon and join us out here in the corridor."

Sweet was a killer. A murderer. He knew how it felt to take a life. You might expect him to be an expert at killing. A man who not only enjoyed taking a life, but a man who didn't fear his bloodlust whatsoever. In this case however, the expression on his face was anything but fearless. If it were humanly possible, I think he would have grabbed his money and run for the hills. But there was no way out of the Crypt. At least no way out without taking the time to unlock that far door, and even then there likely existed another metal door or two to unlock.

He ran into the office, came back out a few seconds later with an M16 and a full mag which he slapped into the automatic rifle's housing. Something had happened in the time it took him to retrieve the weapon and return to the corridor with it. The fear on his gaunt face had been replaced with a kind of determination. There were still beads of sweat covering his forehead, and even more streaks of sweat that ran down his cheeks, droplets that dripped off his chin. It was sweltering inside the concrete cavern of a crypt now that the air conditioning had been blown out. We were all sweating, but Derrick Sweet was hot on the inside and the outside. Maybe he bore a personal grudge against the COs of Dannemora, even the crooked COs who he must have worked closely with down in the Crypt. But when he pulled the slide back on the M16 and shouldered the weapon, I knew then that he was no longer afraid, no longer wanting to run, even if God himself somehow offered him the option to run. He wanted nothing more now than blood. The blood of the COs whose responsibility it was to incarcerate him.

The elevators descended. Within two or three seconds the doors would open, unleashing what I could only assume would be a final assault. Winner take all spoils.

"Okay, gentleman," I said, taking aim. "This is it."

"We do this right," Blood said, "we be outta here in a few minutes. With those kids. Dinner on me."

"You're on, partner," I said. "And don't forget our dates. The girls."

"I just hope they still interested when this thing is finally over."

The elevator doors opened.

"Let 'em have it," I barked as the lights on the Crypt went black.

CHAPTER 46

The pitch dark Crypt lit up with a brilliant display of tracer rounds and red laser beam sites shooting and scooting in the both directions. It was like a series of rapid shooting stars and explosions. There was a kind of beauty to the exchange of gunfire, a kind of choreographed dance of hot red-white light and flashing bullets, the sound of sharp ricochets immediately followed by the spark and flash, and the satisfying pings of metal striking metal, and the thud of lead embedding itself into solid concrete block.

But there was also the scream that came from Derrick Sweet as he charged the two open elevator doors, like a dough boy from a century ago who, having been too afraid even to aim his rifle at the enemy for fear of being exposed and cut down, had now by some miracle been transformed into a fearless man. A man who would sprint the length of no-man's land without regard for his body, as if it were possible for him to retake an enemy trench all on his own. A man with not an ounce of common sense in his blood and bones at all, but only blind determination. And when I heard the last desperate shriek that seemed louder and higher pitched than the others that came before, I knew Derrick Sweet had finally met his maker in the form of a CO's burst of automatic gunfire that struck him in the waist and nearly cut him in two.

Now down flat on my belly, I fired precisely in the direction of the enemy lasers. I knew that Blood, too, had the good sense to position himself in the same way. I emptied one mag, replaced it with a second, emptied that one, and replaced it with a third. By then, the enemy tracers were no longer coming at us, the laser sites no longer bearing down on our chests and heads.

The enemy gunfire had stopped altogether.

The darkness was suddenly replaced not with the bright overhead light, but instead, the eerie red glow of the wall-mounted emergency lighting. The elevator doors closed once more, but this time, there were two men left standing inside the Crypt corridor.

They were Rodney Pappas and his boss, Warden Peter Clark.

CHAPTER 47

The two of them were bathed in the red light. The whites of their eyes reflected the light, as if they weren't human at all, but robotic imitations of the human flesh and blood they once were.

"You seein' what I'm seein'?" Blood said.

"Seeing is believing," I said. "Unless we're as dead as Sweet is, and we're in hell."

The abrupt sound of a metal door burst open came from directly behind us. It was followed by jackboots slapping the floor, automatic weapons locked and loaded.

"Shit," I said. "I should have secured that door from the inside when I had the chance."

"We was gonna use it for our getaway, remember?" Blood said out the corner of his mouth. "It not your fault."

I stole a quick glance over my shoulder, made out the same two beefy bodyguards who had entered my office unannounced just a couple of days ago. Governor Valente's Secret Service bodyguards. Tall, black, hair-trigger-temper goon, Stanley, and shorter goon, Brent. Must be they were sent here to represent their boss: The Honorable Governor Leon Valente. They had their rifles aimed for our backs. Pointblank.

Redirecting my gaze towards the elevators, I eyed the two men making their way along the corridor towards us and I exhaled a sad sigh.

Freedom…how did the old song go? So close but yet, so far away.

"You can drop your weapons any time now," came the booming, nervous voice of Warden Clark. "These men might be able to deadlift a locomotive apiece, but they have sensitive hair triggers."

"We gotta listen to him?" Blood whispered over his shoulder.

"He's the warden," I said. "Everyone listens to the warden. Take it from me."

Blood dropped his M16. I dropped mine.

"Hands up, asshole," uttered a deep voice from behind me.

"Who was that?" I said. "Stanley? That you, honey?"

I felt the sharp, painful jab of a gun barrel in the small of my back.

"Stanley!" Clark shouted. "That's quite enough for now. You'll have your shot at these two in a few moments."

Clark stopped in his tracks. Maybe thirty feet separated him from us. Meanwhile, Rodney, armed with a prison-issue M16, stood his ground only a few feet behind him. Laid out on the painted concrete floor only a few feet away in a pool of his own crimson blood was Derrick Sweet.

"You fucked up," Clark said. "You were supposed to deliver Derrick Sweet and Reginald Moss to Valente personally down in Albany.

Deliver them to him alive and unharmed. You had a private contract."
He cocked his shoulder, then smirked. "Okay, maybe our esteemed
governor would have accepted them a little beat up or even wounded.
But the point is, you not only failed to keep them alive, you poked
your respective noses into something that is most definitely none of
your business. Since when did you go from private dick to vested law
enforcement professional, Mr. Marconi?" He spread out his arms, as if
to draw our attention to the destroyed Crypt. "Now this."

The strange thing was how he smiled after he said it. It was the
kind of smile you expressed after a job well done. A satisfied smile,
a proud smile. The smile of the gambler when he was on a winning
streak. It hit me then, that yes, I did indeed fuck up by not delivering
Moss and Sweet alive. Because by not doing so, I played right into
Clark's, Rodney's, and the governor's grimy hands.

I recalled what Moss had said to me down inside the burning
shelter.

*"He sent you, didn't he? The governor? He sent you personally. Bet he
wants me alive just so he can make sure without a doubt that I'm dead.
Dead and so very fucking silent."*

"You know something, Clark," I said, "I think you're happy Sweet
and Moss are dead. I think that was your intention all along. Like most
politicians, Valente said one thing, but meant something else entirely,
which is just another way of lying. You and he knew full well that if
the FBI, or the state troopers, or the sheriff, or the fucking Mod Squad
located and captured the two cons, they stood the chance of being
reincarcerated unharmed. Relatively speaking anyway. And unharmed
cons have big mouths. Unharmed cons who break out and face life
imprisonment after being caught chirp like birds. But by hiring me to

go after them, you knew they'd put up a fight, and that chances were, they wouldn't live through it. And even if they did, you would have figured out a way to make them dead before the cops got to them. You'd simply blame their unfortunate deaths on me. Me and my partner, Blood."

"Mod Squad?" Blood mumbled.

"Hey," I whispered over my shoulder, "I'm on a roll here."

The smile on Clark's face grew even wider, prouder, more satisfied.

"You're smarter than I give you credit for, Mr. Marconi," he said, clapping his hands together. "Bravo. Bravo indeed."

"You're not going to get away with it," I said. "Dead or alive, those two cons are still going to sing like a tweety bird. You should know that the FBI and Sheriff Hylton are already on their way. You're as good as busted. Valente can hide his head in the sand down in Albany. But he's as good as busted. And did I mention we have pictures of you and Rodney attacking Maude inside her pantry? She was a simple, gentle artist. Wouldn't hurt a flea. And she was also Sheriff Hylton's godmother, which makes her family. The sheriff won't rest until you clowns fall. So why not just put down your weapons and we can all walk out of here alive."

"No one else has to die," Blood added.

Clark smiled, shot a glance over his shoulder at Rodney. Both men smiled back. Rodney gripped his rifle, flexed his muscles, the blue veins in his forearms popping out like live eels caught inside paper thin skin.

"Can I just blow them two away now?" he said.

Clark pulled a pack of smokes from his jacket pocket, lit one up.

"Yes, indeed," he said, exhaling a stream of blue smoke. "I see no reason in the world not to dispose of these two troublemakers immediately, then get on with the business of cleaning this place up and getting our operation back up and running. I'm already fielding calls from Florence ADX SuperMax in Colorado, and Pelican Bay SuperMax in California wondering why communications have ceased."

"So tell me, Clark," I said. "I know why you'd sell your soul. And I know why musclebound Pappas here would sell whatever soul he's got. But why, in your less than humble opinion, would Valente do it? What makes a man in a vaulted position like him abandon every moral fiber in his body to do something so rock bottom as force kids into the sex slave trade? Running meth wasn't good enough for him?"

"We're all slaves in one way or another, Marconi," he said. "And you might say Valente was doing these children a favor. We are all doing them a favor. You see, we pulled them off the street. Gave them food and shelter. A warm bed at night. In return for our kindness we required they make a movie or two. Or perhaps entertain certain customers of our choosing."

"Stop it, warden," Blood said. "You making my head hurt with your spin. You a piece of garbage for what you did to those kids. They carry that shit with them the rest of their days. Lots more days than you got left. Question is, why? You jerks got everything in the world. Money, prestige, and power. Why go to the dark side?"

"Excellent *Star Wars* reference, Blood," I said. Then, over my shoulder, "Wasn't it Stanley?"

Another poke of the gun barrel into my ribs. It stung like hell. Enough to bring tears to my eyes. But I tried my best to maintain a smile and a positive outlook.

Clark smoked his cigarette and assumed the calm, cool expression of a professional state delegate about to address a televised press conference.

"These are all valid questions, Blood," he said. "But sometimes prestige is not enough. And sometimes, there's not enough money. Not as much as people think anyway. And as far as political power goes, I can assure you, Valente is not nearly as powerful as Johnny Q. Public might assume. In fact, the President of the United States of America is not nearly as all powerful and omniscient as the world seems to perceive him. There are other, far more powerful figures at play. The people who pull the strings. You see, Mr. Blood, me and other's like me, we're just puppets. Which is why some men in Governor Valente's position might aspire to the presidency, but he chooses instead to utilize the office of the Governor of the Empire State of New York for far different purposes. And that's to become one of the select few who truly make the decisions, and who truly run this country. And that takes not millions of dollars, but billions." Raising his right arm, index finger extended in the direction of the vault. "That money inside that big metal safe, that's nothing. That's pocket change. What we have going on in America right now, right under the noses of the average working class hero, is a network of Crypt-like operations that are making billions per year. And the beauty of our model isn't trickle-down economics, but instead, trickle up. When my time as warden is done, and Valente's term as governor is done, we'll join a fraternity of a few good men who will set the course of this great nation for now and the future."

"Wow," I said, "I think that brought a tear to my eye. I would clap if I wasn't holding my hands over my head." Then, under my breath, "Blood, what we have here is one twisted and entirely delusional son of bitch."

"You got that right," Blood mumbled.

"We need to hurry," Rodney said, his muscles growing tighter and more tense so that they bulged to the point of bursting under his too tight work shirt. "We need to clean this place out, dispose of the bodies, and dispose of these two assholes now. Can we do that please, Warden Clark?"

"Agreed, Rodney," Clark said as he puffed away on what remained of his cigarette. "I don't like being down here with those creepy orange children inside that room. I wish we could just dispose of them as well. Be done with them already. Eradicate their memory. Their existence."

"He an evil man," Blood said under his breath. "All three of them evil…as evil as evil on earth gets."

"This is your show now, Rodney," Clark said, tossing the cigarette butt onto the floor. "This is your prison after all, and I must respect that, even if you did fuck up with Moss and Sweet by allowing them to escape in the first place. Can you imagine if the two of them had ratted out our operation to the press? Now that would have been the end of everything. Lucky for us all, Mr. Blood and Mr. Marconi also fucked up and those two morons ended up very dead before they could open their respective traps." He peered at the two goons behind us. "Stanley, you and your pal, Brent, please carry on with the execution."

One goon came around Blood's left shoulder and the second one came around my right shoulder.

"Back's up against the wall," Stanley insisted, his automatic rifle barrel aimed for my chest. He was grinning, sneering, tasting my blood even before it was spilled.

Slowly, Blood and I back-stepped until we felt the cold, hard, bullet-pocked wall pressed up against our spines. Just then, my eye caught something. Stepping out of the kitchen area, a boy of no more than thirteen or fourteen, dressed only in his loose orange jumper, his body barely illuminated in the red glow. And then a boy behind him and a girl behind him. I couldn't be certain of what it was they were holding in their hands, but it looked like kitchen knives and forks.

"Blood," I whispered over my shoulder, "you remember Bruce Lee? How bad ass he was? You recall that final fight scene in *Enter the Dragon*? Or was it *Fists of Fury*? You know, where those two huge goons have him backed up against a wall and it looks like curtains for the hero."

"You thinking *Game of Death*," Blood said. "Bruce and Karreem Abdul Jabar go at it. Proof that size don't matter. That skill mean everything."

"Why don't you two shut the fuck up," Stanley said, his index finger sliding onto the trigger. Goon number two mimicked his movements precisely.

"Ready!" Clark shouted, acting the role of the executioner.

Over their shoulder, I made out no less than a dozen knife-and fork-wielding kids sneaking up on Rodney and Clark. I once heard a man say he'd rather fight a Navy Seal than five angry kindergartners. Right now, a dozen furious teenagers armed with kitchen implements were about take out two grown men. All I needed was to stall the two goons for another second.

"Aim," barked Clark.

The two goons tightened their grips on their weapons and improved their stance by spreading their feet shoulder-width apart, legs slightly bent at the knees, index fingers already depressing the triggers. At this range, they'd blow our brains out.

"Okay, Blood," I said under my breath. "When I give the signal, we go all *Game of Death* on these two. You go high, I go low."

"Fire!" Clark ordered.

But Clark didn't get the word out before the kids plunged their knives and forks into his and Rodney's backs. The two men screamed, fell to their knees, the blood spurting out of their wounds. It was enough to distract our firing squad for a very necessary and welcome beat.

"Now, Blood!" I insisted while dropping onto my hands, swinging my legs around like a whip, taking Stanley out at the ankles so that he fell hard onto his side, the rounds spraying out of his M16 and connecting only with the block wall and the ceiling.

Blood thrust himself forward, slapped the automatic rifle out of Brent's hands with such force, it slammed against the far wall. He then wrapped his left arm around the goon's head and, quickly thrusting it upwards and sideways, snapped his neck in two as if it were a pretzel stick. Blood dropped the now dead Brent onto the concrete, just as I disarmed Stanley, thrusting the stock down onto his cranial cap, crushing it like an egg.

By the time I raised up my head, I saw that Rodney and Clark were down on their bellies, their bodies as still as corpses, no less than a half dozen knives and forks sticking out of their backs.

Once more I stuck my fingers in my mouth and whistled. Having grabbed hold of their attention, the kids stopped and stood stone stiff. Beneath them, bleeding out on the concrete floor, were two out of the three men who were responsible for their incarceration, their slavery, their abuse.

"It's over," I said. "The killing is over."

Realizing what they'd just accomplished, and the grisly results of it, a few of the kids began to cry. I let them cry it out for a time, while Blood and I caught our breath. I thanked God we were alive to see another day. I thanked God we lived long enough to free the kids.

CHAPTER 48

Moments later, the kids had once more composed themselves. Having asked them to grab up their cash-filled shopping bags including the one Sweet had filled for himself, Blood and I approached the metal door at the back of the office. This time I used a key I took off of Rodney to unlock the door. It was a ten-flight hike up the concrete and metal-pan stairs, but no one seemed to mind. By the time we arrived at the top, we were drenched in sweat, but at least we were alive to appreciate it.

I unlocked the exterior door with the same key, pushed it open. Then, telling everyone to maintain silence, I told them to follow me back around the corner of the laundry facility. We made it without a hitch to where my 4Runner was still parked beside the same laundry truck. Without having to say a word, Blood immediately proceeded to pile the kids and their cash bags into the back of the laundry truck. He then hopped out, pulled the bay overhead door down, and secured the metal latch.

"Let's just hope the keys still in it," he said.

"What if they're not?"

"Take me a second or two to hot wire. No sweat."

He hopped up into the truck, took his place behind the wheel.

"Keys" he said, smiling. Smiling was a rare event for Blood and it was a pleasure to see since it often meant we were about to get away with our lives. In this case, our lives and the lives of some innocent kids.

Snatching up Sweet's cash bag from out of the laundry truck, I got in the 4Runner, fired it up, pulled out of the parking spot. Driving back towards the guard house at the top of the service entrance, I peered into the rearview mirror and was relieved to see that Blood was right on my tail. When I came to the guard house, I stopped. Lucas was still situated on the floor on his backside, bound by the gray duct tape.

I grabbed the extra money bag that belonged to Sweet, tied the handles tightly together, tossed it to him.

"Your cut, Lucas," I said. "Plus interest."

He mumbled something, but it was impossible to make out with that gag covering his mouth.

I hung a right out of the parking lot in the direction of the Clinton County Jail, just as an army of state trooper prowlers blew past us, converging on the prison entrance, the short, stocky, Vincent D'Amico plainly visible in my rear view mirror, leading the charge as he exited the lead vehicle. In the end, we made it out of the prison with the kids and their cash, with barely seconds to spare.

CHAPTER 49

No less than a half dozen black Chevy Suburbans pull up to the front gates of the Governor's Mansion on Eagle Street in downtown Albany. The four-wheel drive vehicles are alive with red, white, and blue LED flashers and ear-piercing sirens. The dark suited FBI agents pile out and, service weapons gripped in their hands, approach the bullet-proof glass enclosed guard house and demand entry. Without hesitation, the guard manning the booth opens the front gates. The FBI jump back into their vehicles and storm up the drive.

At the same time, a chopper arrives on the scene. It belongs to a local news channel that is filming the scene live. The chopper beams a bright white spotlight down on the compound while it flies one circle after another, scoring brilliant visuals of the black Suburbans racing not only up the drive, but also on the lawn, barreling through neatly trimmed shrubbery and flattening several exterior lamp posts.

Arriving at the house, the agents manning the lead Suburban spot *a man climbing out a second floor window. It's the governor. He jumps down onto a porch overhang that wraps around the old stone structure. Standing precariously on the edge of the overhang, he looks over his shoulder at the coming onslaught of federal agents, and he jumps.*

Now down on his back, writhing in pain, Governor Valente screams. It's not the pain that's so offensive, but the way the shattered, jagged femur on his left leg sticks out of his pant leg.

The FBI agents quickly descend upon him, yank him up, and pulling his arms behind his back, handcuff him.

"I need a fucking hospital!" he screams.

"You'll get all the medical attention you require as soon as we read you your rights, governor," the lead agent insists. "But from this point on, it's probably best that you keep your mouth shut."

Shoved into the back seat of the first Suburban, the governor is then led back down the drive to the front gates, where an army of journalists have descended upon the Eagle Street entrance. Forced to stop or else run the media darlings down, the lead agent behind the wheel demands they disperse immediately. But the open window is looked upon as an opportunity for a few select journalists to stick their heads inside and boldly shout out questions for the fallen career politician.

One of these journalists is Tanya Rucker, who has only arrived on the scene from upstate ten minutes ago.

Shoving her hand held mic into the open window, she barks, "Governor, why'd you do it?" It's a simple question that carries the same weight as if she had the time to pose, "Governor, why did you betray the sanctity of your office? Why did you betray the people you govern? Why did you so willingly abuse those kids? Why did you elect to enter into a drug ring that's connected to identical drug rings inside prisons all over the country? Why be such an absolute fucking reprehensible asshole when you had the political world at your fingertips?"

For a long beat, the Suburban interior goes as quiet as a morgue at midnight. There is only the question posed and the mic shoved inside the open window begging for an answer.

"No comment," Governor Leon Valente whispers after a time.

With that the agent pushes Rucker back with his forearm, and electronically rolls up the window. Triggering the sirens, he pulls out into the crowd, forcing the mob to step aside. Not a single word is spoken all the way to the Albany Medical Center emergency room.

CHAPTER 50

That night, as the sun settled on the Adirondack Park, we sat around a corner dining room table at Fangs, the remains of several different Chinese dishes taking up space beside two bottles of red wine. One of them empty, the second nearly drained.

"Well, we finally get to have dinner with two fine-looking ladies," Blood said.

"That your way of making a toast, Blood?" I said, shooting a wink at both Betty and Bridgette, both of whom looked ravishing in their loose skirts and loose summer-weight tops. Betty sat beside Blood, so close to him, her shoulder was rubbing up against his thick bicep which protruded from his tight black T-shirt like a mountain with a high, round peak.

My date was sitting close to me too, but not that close. She was, however, resting her hand on my thigh. Something I not only enjoyed, but that filled me with warmth and happiness. It was the way it used to be with Fran whenever she would touch me.

I raised up my glass.

"To the two best dates in Dannemora," I said.

Bridgette shot Betty a look, then laughed.

"I think we'll take that as a compliment," she said.

We clinked glasses making sure everyone looked everyone in the eye or else break the spell of the toast.

"You see," Blood said, drinking a swallow of wine, "Keeper means well. But he don't know how to talk to women. Why he's always lonely."

I drank some wine. It was beginning to make me feel slightly tipsy. Something I usually avoided these days. But it was an evening for celebrating. We'd managed to free a whole bunch of kids and pay for some of their college tuitions while we were at it. Maybe we had a chance to score some real cash for ourselves, but Blood and I played by the rules. Rather, we liked to think that the rules we played by were above the law.

The door opened behind us and two people walked in. They were dressed in black suits and sunglasses, even though the summer sun had all but set on the horizon.

Agents Doyle and Muscolino.

They approached our table, not like they were pleasantly surprised to see us, but more like they knew we were here the entire time.

"Don't look now," Blood said. "But we got some spooks on our tail."

"I love it when you say spook," I said.

The two agents stood over our table.

"Evening, Mr. Marconi, Mr. Blood," Muscolino said. Then, eyeing our dates, "Good evening, ladies."

Everyone mumbled a polite good evening back at him.

"You're still wearing sunglasses," I said.

"Excuse me?" he said.

"I said you're still wearing your sunglasses. It's dark out now and you're indoors. You know what they call people who wear sunglasses indoors?"

"No, what do they call them?"

"Jerks," I said.

Maintaining his stone-face, Muscolino slowly removed his Ray-Bans. Agent Doyle, taking his cue, did the same.

"There," he said, "now we're not jerks."

"So to what do we owe the pleasure?" Blood said.

"We apologize for the intrusion, but we need to talk. I've got a team of agents on their way and we're going to require some extensive interviews with you and the major players in the basement operation at Dannemora. The, what do they call it, the Crypt?"

"Sounds serious," Bridgette said.

"Federal investigation's always a serious matter, ma'am," Doyle said.

"I just love shows 'bout Federal Agents," Betty said while brushing back her thick red hair with her open hand. "I just love *X-Files* reruns." She laughed. "That's what you two look like. Like Agent Scully and Agent Mulder."

"We get that a lot, ma'am," Muscolino said.

I looked at my watch. "Well, agents, it's going on nine o'clock. We're already a little drunk, and you're not going to get very far with us tonight. So why not take a seat and have a drink."

Muscolino turned to Doyle, gave her a look like, *Well, what do you think?*

"Sounds like a plan to me," she said. "My feet are killing me from walking around all day."

"Okay, agreed," Muscolino said as he pulled out a chair and sat himself down. "Maybe we'll find something interesting to talk about. Governor Valente's arrest for one, or haven't you guys seen the TV?"

"Read about it on my smartphone," I said. "Still can't get over his trying to run away like that. Where the hell did he think he was going to go? Mexico?"

"Desperate times call for desperate measures, Keeper." He nodded at Blood. "The State of New York owes you two quite a debt for what you did. You put your lives on the line and exposed a multi-billion-dollar crime syndicate that extends way beyond state borders."

"You saying someone should offer me a raise, Agent Muscolino?"

"If I were your boss, I would most definitely reevaluate your stock value. But then, you're your own boss."

Blood raised up his hands to get the waitress's attention. "Two more glasses," he said, "and another bottle."

She brought both right away, opening the bottle at the table. Blood poured the agents some wine and we all made another toast to closing the Crypt. Then, Agent Muscolino pulled out his notebook.

"Mind if I just ask a few simple questions while we we're sitting here?"

"I don't see why not," I said. "We're heroes after all."

"Down inside the Crypt vault we found several stacks worth upwards of five million dollars US apiece. Quite an extraordinary sum for an operation of its size down in the prison basement. One of the stacks was missing some bundles from it. Not a whole lot, in relative terms, but enough for us to take notice. Do you have any idea where the money could have disappeared to?"

I looked at Blood. He looked at me, shrugged his shoulders.

"Beats me," I said. "Beats him too."

Muscolino looked down at his lap, then looked up again. He sighed.

"That's all you have to say on the subject?" he said.

I might have done the right thing, told him that after we delivered the children to the emergency room at the Champlain Valley Physicians Hospital Medical Center, Blood and I stuffed the cash bags into five separate lockers at the old Grayhound bus station. But sometimes you had to do the wrong thing in order to preserve the greater good.

"Yup," I said. "That's all I have to say."

"Will you come to my office tomorrow and swear under oath that you, in fact, do not know what happened to the money?"

"Yup."

"Even if it means a federal offense should I find out you are lying?"

"Yup."

"Even if one or more of those kids spills the beans when the hospital staff at Champlain Valley gives us the green light to interview them?"

"Yup."

"You gonna keep saying yup to every question I ask?"

"Yup and maybe nope."

Muscolino smiled. He had a nice smile it turned out. Life was serious sometimes. But not always. I preferred the latter.

"I repeat," he said. "Anything you say can and will be held against you in a court of law, even if you say it in Fangs. Yups and nopes included."

"Yup," I said, suddenly recalling something that might be of interest to him. Digging in my pocket, I pulled out the Post-it-Note with the smiley Chinese face drawn on it. I handed it to him. "Valente attached this to my advance check," I added. "I guess it was his way of making a funny."

Muscolino looked at it contemplatively for a long beat before stuffing it in the breast pocket on his jacket.

He drank some wine, jotted something down in his notebook.

"Next question," he said. "How's the Moogoo Gai Pan here?"

"Exquisite," Bridgette said.

"The best in Dannemora," I said.

"I love it," Betty said.

"Let's get drunk," Blood said.

We proceeded to do exactly that.

THE END

ABOUT THE AUTHOR

Vincent Zandri is the *New York Times* and *USA Today* bestselling author of more than twenty-five novels, including *Everything Burns, The Innocent, The Remains, Orchard Grove,* and *The Shroud Key.* His novel *Moonlight Weeps* won both the International Thriller Writers Award and the Shamus Award. He is also the author of the Shamus Award nominated Dick Moonlight PI series. A freelance photojournalist and solo traveler, he is the founder of the blog *The Vincent Zandri Vox.* His books *Orchard Grove* and *The Scream Catcher* are currently available from Polis Books. He lives in Albany, New York. Visit him online at www.VincentZandri.com or on Twitter at @VincentZandri.